Autumn Always Comes

HEARTLINES

Books by Pam Lyons

A Boy Called Simon
He Was Bad
It Could Never Be ...
Latchkey Girl
Danny's Girl

Books by Anita Eires

Tug Of Love
Summer Awakening
Spanish Exchange
Star Dreamer
Californian Summer

Books by Mary Hooper

Love Emma XXX
Follow That Dream
My Cousin Angie

Books by Barbara Jacobs

Two Times Two

Books by Jane Pitt

Loretta Rose
Autumn Always Comes

Books by Ann de Gale

Island Encounter

Heartlines

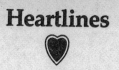

Jane Pitt

Autumn Always Comes

A Pan Original

First published 1984 by Pan Books Ltd,
Cavaye Place, London SW10 9PG
9 8 7 6 5 4 3 2
© Jane Pitt 1984
ISBN 0 330 28442 8
Phototypeset by Input Typesetting Ltd, London
Printed in Great Britain by
Hunt Barnard Printing, Aylesbury, Bucks

Getting There

The plane turned slowly and she looked down at the collection of dolls' houses and miniature duck ponds. The Thames seemed to snake gracefully through them all like a calm silver ribbon, as if it were tying them up and turning them into an enormous, magical present.

The *No Smoking* sign flashed on. People fumbled with seatbelts, packed away paperbacks and magazines, and above the roar of the engines conversation seemed to hum and ripple.

She looked down through the cabin window again at the toy-town, wondering what it would be like to really live there for six whole weeks.

She'd read about England, of course. Everybody had to read about it at school.

She knew, for example, it was a constitutional monarchy; that London was the capital with more than seven million people living in it; that the currency was the pound sterling, the main agricultural products dairy farming, livestock and fishing – and that her mother wanted her to bring home a lambswool sweater and some jars of marmalade. But none of that made it seem any more touchable, and she shivered suddenly – a sick feeling that had nothing to do with the plane's dropping altitude grabbing hold of her.

She'd been away from home before, of course. Last summer she'd spent a fortnight in Mallorca with Katerine. And the summer before that, when she was only fourteen, she and Dolores Camino had actually been allowed to go on a school trip to Madrid.

But that was different. Katerine and Dolores were

friends. She'd known them and their families all her life. They talked the same language and understood the same jokes. In the spring holidays she and Dolores had even fallen in love with the same boy.

In England, in London, there would only be Sandie to talk to – whom she'd written to, but never met.

The sick feeling turned to near panic.

She'd boasted such a lot about the English trip and told everybody how she'd think of them doing the same old boring summer things while she was busy shopping in the King's Road and waving to Prince Charles.

Now it was all here and all happening, and as the Iberia plane touched down and began to trundle along the runway she took a deep breath, crossed her fingers and muttered, '¡Buena suerte!'

Chapter 1

'Juana Alvarez?' The voice seemed to float out from the middle of a huddle of people all wearing dull jackets and anxious expressions. 'Are you there? Have you arrived? Did you,' it almost pleaded, 'get off that plane?'

It was impossible to tell who was actually speaking and I peered round worriedly, part of me wishing I could run away and hide somewhere. Then I straightened my shoulders, took a deep breath and a half-step forward and said, '*Si?*', smiling blindly in the direction of all the jackets.

If only the voice would grow a body and walk towards me I'd be all right, I reasoned hopefully. It was a nice voice that sounded as if it laughed a lot, and I searched desperately for its owner, feeling as anxious and bewildered as everybody else. 'It is I. I am here. By the orange rubbish bin.'

Despite myself I almost giggled. It wasn't the way I'd imagined landing in England at all, because being by an orange rubbish bin full of hamburger wrappings and plastic straws simply didn't seem to be the most exciting or romantic way to start a holiday.

'Thank goodness!' Somebody shouldered their way through the dull jackets and I gasped and blinked, wondering if I was still asleep on the plane. 'I didn't think I was ever going to find you in this mob. I'm sorry I'm late.'

A slim, slightly suntanned hand with broken nails reached across and picked up my basket and coat. I followed the line of the hand back to the face and gulped again. It was vaguely familiar – and absolutely gorgeous!

'It took me ages to park,' he went on. 'Then I went to the wrong terminal because none of us could remember which one it was and we think Elvira's eaten your last letter.'

'Elvira?' I had to almost run to keep up with him as he marched through the crowds.

'You'll meet her in a bit. She's a dog. She's not sure what *kind* of a dog. She gets a bit confused. Some days she thinks she's a cat, or an elephant. It seems to depend on the weather and how many yeast tablets she's had. Anyhow,' he slowed down to avoid an airport trolley and grinned at me, 'she nicks things. So be warned. Don't leave anything you even vaguely value lying around! Now where the devil's Maggie got to?'

'Maggie?' My head was spinning. If Elvira was a dog who thought she was an elephant, Maggie was probably a bicycle who thought she was a racing car.

'Girlfriend. Oh heck!' He skidded to a stop suddenly and looked at me in embarrassment. 'I'm sorry. I haven't even introduced myself. I'm Barry Walker. Sandie's brother.'

'Yes.' I'd guessed already. Sandie and I had been penfriends for two years so I'd seen photographs of her family. 'I almost recognised you. From your pictures,' I explained, feeling muddled.

'Good grief!' he laughed, grabbing me by the arm and hustling me towards the luggage arrivals. 'You mean you could make sense of them? Nobody in our family can ever get anything in focus. In fact, it's a miracle when they don't cut your head off!

'*There's* Maggie!' he exploded suddenly. 'Over by the shop. Why on earth didn't she do what I asked and stay in this corner? Women!' he snorted, waving to her impatiently. 'I don't know how any of them manage to live as long as they do! Most of them are more scatterbrained than Elvira, and she's got an excuse. She's a dog and nobody's liberated them yet!'

I gaped at him, my mouth opening and closing like a goldfish taking in air. None of his thoughts seemed directly connected to each other, and although Sandie had once explained to me that Barry was twenty and almost a genius I had to keep making mental leaps to understand what he was talking about.

'*Maggie!*' he bellowed. 'Move it, love! I'm over here. I've found Juana!'

'Juanita,' I corrected him shyly. 'Juana means "Joan".'

'What does Juanita mean, then?' Perhaps I was being unfair, but the new voice didn't sound as if it *ever* laughed. In fact it crackled the way ice cubes do when you drop them into slightly warm liquid.

'Little Joan, at a guess, dumbo!' Barry threw an arm round Maggie's shoulders and gave her a quick hug. 'And what's up with you? I wasn't gone *that* long. I've told you before, if the wind changes your face'll stay that way, and it doesn't suit you!' He ran a finger lightly across the angry frown lines between her eyes.

'You *know* what's up,' she pouted at him, ignoring me completely. 'We were supposed to go shopping this afternoon, not spend hours trolling round Heathrow looking for sixteen-year-old tourists! Why couldn't your mum and dad have come? She's *their* responsibility. Or Sandie? She could've caught the tube and met her. It's nothing to do with you, is it?'

I turned the other way and pretended I wasn't

listening. Barry's girlfriend was very, very pretty — and very, very sulky!

'Dad's working, so he's got the car. Mum won't drive mine since she reversed into the dustbins and dented the bumper. And Sandie had to go to the dentist.' He turned quickly to me and smiled. 'She *hates* going to the dentist, even though he is a friend of the family. So far she's broken the same appointment six times. Dad gave her an ultimatum this morning. Either she went this afternoon before Bob goes on holiday so she could smile at you with perfectly be-e-autiful teeth,' he pulled his own mouth back at the corners as far as it would go, 'or she took Elvira to have her toenails clipped.

'All in all, she sensibly decided it'd be less painful to go and see Bob, although the fact that young Robin was likely to be around the surgery *could* just have been the thing that swayed her!'

I thought about that, following the other two through the crowds. Sandie had mentioned Robin sometimes in her letters. She was keen on him, but he seemed to spend most of his time playing cricket and ignoring her. She'd *never* mentioned Elvira, though — or her toenails.

We collected my suitcases and began to follow the arrows towards the exit. Barry shifted my smaller case to under his arm and took Maggie's hand. I couldn't help noticing that he squeezed it reassuringly, and I suddenly felt terribly in the way.

Barry Walker wasn't at all what I'd expected. Somehow I'd imagined he'd wear spectacles and have a stoop and a permanent sniff, like Carlos — the genius in my class back home.

And Maggie, with her long blonde hair, tight miniskirt and endless legs just made me feel a fat, foolish foreigner.

I flicked my hair out of my eyes and swallowed hard. Spain and all its familiar things suddenly seemed much, much more than two hours away and I clutched the new leather handbag Mama and Papa had given me closer.

'Don't worry, Juanita,' Mama had sat on the edge of my bed only yesterday and said softly. 'The Walkers sound nice. Papa likes them, and it's a wonderful opportunity for you. Six weeks in another country!'

'Yes, but Mama,' I'd started playing with the ragdoll I'd had ever since I'd been a baby, '*school*! In England! To learn English! Why? I know enough. I can speak okay.'

'Of course you can! But you'll learn more. It'll help you with your exams. Maybe one day you'll even go to college in England. And anyhow,' she'd smoothed the sheets down, 'Papa wants it for you. He's so proud of you and he wants you to be *better* than anyone else. Better than Katerine and Dolores and all your other friends.'

'I know, I know,' I'd sighed. 'But if I get homesick? If I don't *like* the school? If the Walkers don't like me?'

'Then if it's *so* bad,' she'd patted my hand, 'you telephone and we arrange for you to come home. But a summer in England, Juanita! It'll be wonderful! I wish I'd had the chance when I was your age.'

But she hadn't and I had, and as Barry's old car finally pulled away from the airport and headed in towards London I looked out at the unfamiliar, green countryside.

'All right in the back, Juanita?' Barry asked cheerfully. 'Sorry it isn't a Rolls or anything, but we impoverished students have to make the best of what we've got, and although she looks as if she's falling apart, I'm very fond of her!'

For a second I wondered if he was talking about Maggie again and glanced at her, but she was staring ahead through the windscreen as if she had a very nasty smell under her nose. Then I realised he must've meant the car and giggled quietly to myself as I wound down the window a little.

'Too hot?' He glanced round at me quickly.

'Y-yes.' I made my face stop giggling at the thought of Maggie falling apart. 'Sandie's letter said to bring sweaters and things, but it seems warmer here than Spain!'

'Well, make the most of it!' The car was bumbling noisily through the motorway traffic. 'It'll probably snow tomorrow, eh, Maggie?'

'Oh Barry, honestly!' Maggie tossed her head impatiently. 'It *never* snows in summer! Don't be so childish! The weather forecast says the heatwave's going to continue, which means,' she sighed and fanned herself with a fold-up map, 'I can stop going to the solarium and start getting tanned properly.'

'Well, whoopee for that!' Barry grunted sarcastically, slowing down as the tail-back of traffic thickened.

I huddled into my seat, wishing I hadn't spoken. The last thing I wanted on my first evening was to cause an argument, and from the tone of Barry's voice that was precisely what was happening.

Maggie snapped, 'Anyway, we've had a *ruined* afternoon, we're supposed to be going to Ray's barbecue tonight. It's already half-past four and I haven't even had my bath yet. I don't know how on *earth* you expect me to be ready on time!' She tapped her long scarlet fingernails against the dashboard and sighed, while I tried to make myself seem even smaller.

'I've got news for you,' Barry's own voice had turned icy, 'I don't give a damn whether you're ready on time or not, Maggie! In fact,' he pulled off the motorway and followed a signpost towards somewhere called Putney, 'you can eat your burned sausages all on your own! I'm not coming to Ray's. I've just decided.'

He glanced at her, his hands gripping the wheel tightly. 'You are rude, self-centred, and a pain! Talking to Elvira's more entertaining than talking to *you*! I'll drop you at the tube station. Okay?'

She swung sideways to look at him, her hair floating out behind her like a thick wedding-veil, and I concentrated on counting the number of stitches it had taken to appliqué the pattern on the flap of my bag.

'If that's how you feel, Barry Walker,' she almost squawked, 'you can stop and let me out right now!'

'It'll be a pleasure, sweetheart!' He pulled over to the side of the road and the car almost skidded to a halt. 'Have a nice hitch all the way to Wimbledon!'

If I'd been Barry I think I'd have just shrivelled up at the glance she threw at him, and after she'd gone – slamming her door so loudly the entire windscreen seemed to shake – I half-expected him to turn round and tell *me* what a pain I was for messing up his afternoon. But he didn't. He leaned back in his seat and roared with laughter.

'Come on, little Joan!' Barry turned and grinned. 'Hop in the front and let's go and see Sandie's new fillings!'

I clambered out nervously, hoping I could sink gracefully into the passenger seat the way Maggie had done at Heathrow and impress him. But of course I got myself all muddled up in the seatbelt she'd left snaking across the clutter on the floor.

'I – I'm awfully sorry if this is my fault,' I stammered, blushing like a ripe tomato as he gently untwisted me and settled me into place. 'Perhaps she'll ring you later?' *I* would've done!

'To be perfectly honest, Juanita,' he reached across and gave me a friendly pat, then tested the door to make sure I'd closed it properly, 'I don't care if I don't see her till Christmas! We've been on-again off-again for months now, and let's face it – she *was* being a spoiled brat, wasn't she?'

'But she's very beautiful.' The way he used words puzzled me. 'And if she'd planned your day . . .'

'I sometimes think the Maggies of this world are only beautiful on the outside, and then only when it suits them,' he grunted, sounding a lot older than he was and watching the traffic in his mirror. 'The day they wake up to the fact that they actually care about something more than their nail-varnish and next hairdressing appointment is the day they start growing up.' He pulled carefully out into the stream of cars. 'Though why I should be talking to you like this, I can't imagine!'

Neither could I, but as he started to whistle under his breath I felt myself begin to relax. Of the first two people I'd met in England, one seemed to be a friend, so maybe things weren't going to be too bad after all!

Chapter 2

We didn't talk much for the rest of the journey. Barry spent a lot of time shouting at other drivers through his open window, and humming Sting's 'Spread a Little Happiness' under his breath.

I just watched the shops and streets and tall grey buildings, and tried to stop myself yawning.

It was either the unexpected heat, or the excitement, or the fact that I hadn't slept much last night, but I suddenly felt heavy with tiredness.

'Next turning!' he grunted eventually, waving cheerfully to an old lady weighed down with plastic carrier-bags.

I pressed my nose against the window, trying to ignore the bubble of excitement that had started to grow up somewhere between my stomach and my chest.

On one side of the road were tall houses, squashed together as if they'd landed there by accident.

On the other, for as far as I could see, was pale yellowish-green grass, cropped short and dying because of no rain, and a mixture of small and tall trees muddling together side by side like a kinder-garten child's drawing.

People were sprawled on benches watching their

dogs walking themselves; girls in bikinis were sunbathing on towels as if it were the beach, not the middle of London; and a group of men all in white were playing cricket.

'That's our common.' Barry waited impatiently for the traffic lights to change. 'We're lucky it's so close. At least you can imagine you're actually breathing fresh air when you're in the middle of it! Of course, you've got to get out there before the rush-hour and the diesel fumes start! There are gardens on the other side. And tennis courts. And a boating pond. But I expect Sandie and her mates will introduce you to all that.'

The car juddered to a halt outside a tall thin house with strange criss-crossed glass in its windows and roses rioting in the tiny paved patch of front garden.

'Home!' Barry sighed thankfully, turning off the engine and giving me a quick grin. 'I hate driving at weekends! Everybody's so busy not watching where they're going! Here's Sandie.'

The shiny black front door had been thrown open and a girl about my own age with short curly hair was standing there holding something that looked for all the world like a hairy rug on legs by the collar and waving at me. The rug was shaking itself and barking!

Sandie was shorter than I'd imagined from her photographs and not nearly as elegant as Maggie, I noticed, sighing in relief. In fact, she was what I'd call 'normal', sort of round at the bottom and skinnier on top – like me – as if none of her quite fitted together yet.

'Don't look so petrified!' Barry opened his door and almost dropped on to the pavement. 'She won't bite. Neither will Elvira, come to that! Though she'll probably paw you to death. The dog,' he explained, seeing I was looking confused again, 'not Sandie! I'll dump your cases in the garden then take the car round to the garage.'

'The garage?' I was busy fighting the seatbelt again.

'Mmm. We hire one. It's a couple of blocks away. We were lucky to get it, but it's safer than parking in the street. Joy-riders on a Saturday night and all that, particularly when the fair's here,' he said vaguely.

'Oh.' I undid myself with a 'ping' and carefully opened the passenger door. A garage that you had to *walk* to to get your car from when you had a car in the first place to stop you walking anywhere didn't make a lot of sense to me. But probably, I thought, stretching my back thankfully, I'd misunderstood him again.

'Sandie!' Barry yelled, lifting my case and bag over the gate. 'Stick Elvira in the kitchen and come and give us a hand, there's a good little sister!'

She stuck her tongue out at him, then shooed the dog into the house, closed the door behind her and began to walk towards us. For some reason, I knew she was as nervous as I was.

'Hi!' she grinned, pushing out her hand. 'Shafe journey?'

'Pardon?' I took her hand and shook it, wondering if her face was always so lopsided.

'Sorry!' She rubbed her right cheek. 'Inshection hashn't worn off yet. Had three fillingsh,' she added, as if that explained everything – which it did, more or less.

'Did they hurt?' I asked, following her shyly up the

17

concrete path.

'Fillingsh didn't. Inshections did!'

'Awh, and wasn't Robin there to hold your hand and tell you to be a big, brave girl?' Barry squeezed past us, eyes twinkling affectionately.

'No! He was *not*!' Sandie almost spat, frowning blackly at him. 'In fact, that was a rotten con you and Dad pulled on me! You said his match'd been called off, and it hadn't!'

'No, we didn't,' Barry corrected her. 'We said we didn't know, but he definitely wasn't playing tomorrow so he might be around today. And anyhow,' he opened the door a fraction of an inch and peered through the gap, 'going on about Robin when Juanita's probably dying to go to the loo or something isn't very hospitable, Sandie!'

'Juanita,' Sandie pulled her face down at the edges and it went even more lopsided, 'I'm sho *shorry!* But my *brother*,' she purposefully stood on his foot as she went up the steps to the door, 'is one large *pain!* And if you haven't found that out already, you shoon will! Don't let him fool you with all this scharm,' she almost growled. 'If he *wasn't* my brother I wouldn't even *look* at him!'

I'd just decided that everybody in England seemed to be a pain when Elvira burst through the door with a delighted 'woof!' and started sniffing at me.

'Sandie, I *told* you,' another voice floated towards us sounding slightly irritable, 'to shut Elvira out the back! She's coming into season soon and we really *don't* want every Tom, Dick and Harry of the neighbourhood mongrels serenading us all night!'

Mrs Walker *was* elegant. In fact, you could immediately see the resemblance between Barry and her, right down to the faded blue denims and the suntanned hand that was stretched out towards me.

'Hello, Juanita.' She smiled at me and her entire face seemed to sparkle. She must've been in her mid-forties, but she looked a lot younger. 'Did you have a good flight? Come on in. You must be gasping for a cool drink.

'Sandie,' she turned to her daughter, 'don't just stand there like an idiot! Grab the rest of Juanita's things, and *please*,' she swung round on Barry, 'get that dog inside! According to Mrs Sweete it got into her garden after you left and scared poor little Tiddly-kins half to death. Pity it didn't manage completely!'

'Tiddlykins,' she put an arm round my shoulders and guided me into the hall, 'is the most repulsive cat you have ever met in your life!'

'Tiddly . . .?' Perhaps learning English in school in England wasn't such a bad idea after all! It looked as if it might be the only way I'd ever understand *any* of the Walker family!

'The animal is actually called Octavius Caesar the Third, as you very well know, Anne!' Mr Walker who was tall, grey-haired, and more square — like Sandie — loomed out of the shadows and shook my hand. 'My wife calls the infernal thing Tiddlykins because, well . . .' He trailed off and I heard Sandie explode with laughter behind me.

'What he means,' she giggled as we all went into a long, high-ceilinged kitchen-cum-dining-room, 'is that it does all its business in Mum's garden, usually after she's just planted out a whole load of things!'

'Business?' If Maggie's blisters had blisters by now, my headache was developing a headache! 'A *cat* does business?'

'Yes. *You* know!' Sandie nudged me, still giggling, then made scraping movements with her hands.

'Oh!' I felt my face break into a smile. 'You mean it goes to the toilet! But I still don't understand . . .?'

'Never mind, Juana!' Barry clapped me on the shoulder and I glanced at him gratefully. 'You'll get the hang of everything soon.

'Yes, Mum, I know. I'm going! I'm going! And yes,' he bent and kissed Mrs Walker lightly on the cheek, 'I won't forget to collect the joint from Mr Whyte.

'In the middle of a heatwave,' he explained, while I perched clumsily on the edge of a tall stool, 'Mum has decided, in her infinite wisdom, that we're going to have a full roast-beef lunch tomorrow in your honour. Yorkshire puddings, roast potatoes, horse-radish, the lot! *Robin*,' he screwed up his face mischievously at Sandie and she threw him a dirty look, 'and his parents are coming, too!'

'Pay no attention to my son, Juanita!' Mrs Walker handed me a tall glass of chilled fruit juice. 'Tomorrow's Sunday, so we're having some friends round for Sunday lunch, that's all.'

'I've heard of Yorkshire puddings,' I said shyly. 'You eat them with jam sometimes, don't you? But horses' radishes?'

'It's a root. That you grate and make into a sauce,' Mr Walker tried to explain gently.

'It's horrid!' Sandie hissed. 'Very hot. But Mum says it's traditional. And don't expect *her* Yorkshire puddings to have jam on. She puts salt in 'em!'

'Oh.' I didn't know what else to say. I didn't know what else they *expected* me to say. 'Well,' I gulped the last of my drink, 'I'm sure it will all be very lovely.'

'Let's wait and see!' To my relief Mrs Walker turned away from the sink and smiled at me. 'Now you must be absolutely exhausted, dear. And I'm sure we're all talking much too quickly for you,' she added understandingly, while I smiled, feeling very, very grateful.

'Sandie, take Juanita upstairs and get her settled in to her room. The water's hot if she wants a bath or a shower. We'll have an early supper.' She shot Barry a warning look. 'And I do mean *early*, Barry! Not one of your "I'll be back at half-past six" and suddenly it's eight o'clock episodes!'

'Okay! Okay! I take the hint!' Barry laughed at her in a way I would never dare laugh at *my* mother. 'I'll dump the car, get the meat and then mosey on back to the ol' homestead.' He said the last bit in a terrible American accent that made me giggle, caught my eye and winked.

'Well, before you mosey on off,' Mr Walker drawled, opening a can of beer, 'there's a message for you on the hall pad. Maggie says she doesn't want to see you again – again!'

'Oh.' Barry's face didn't really change. The laugh was still in place, but I had the peculiar cold feeling some kind of shadow had fallen across the back of his eyes. 'And what'm I supposed to do about that?'

An uneasy silence fell over the kitchen.

Mrs Walker fussed with dishes by the sink.

Mr Walker started trying to dent his beer-can with his fingers.

Sandie stared through the low window as if something a lot more serious than Tiddlykins had just walked across the lawn.

Even Elvira stopped thumping her tail against the radiator and sniffing flies.

'Apparently nothing,' Mrs Walker said finally, very quietly. 'Now do go and collect the meat, dear, before Mr Whyte closes. And *Sandie*,' she glared fiercely at her daughter, 'take Juanita upstairs *now*!

'I will never,' she smiled, but I wasn't convinced by her face, 'understand this family! I'm sure yours is different. I'm sure *they* don't have to be told everything at least three times before they move themselves!'

'Th-there is only me to tell,' I gulped, wondering what was going on. The earlier easy atmosphere had thickened into something I felt I could almost touch. 'Papa tells Mama. Mama tells me.' I spread my hands and tried to smile. 'It's very simple.'

'Yes, well, that's more than you can say about here! Sandie, please!' The smile was now lipsticked into position.

'Come on, Juanita.' Sandie tugged me by the sleeve and I got clumsily to my feet, following her back through into the hall.

'Don't worry.' She pulled a sympathetic face and patted me quickly. 'Mum's thinking about having a family crisis, but it isn't your fault!'

'Crisis?' I plodded up the stairs behind her.

'Yes. Because of Barry and Maggie. It always is,' she added darkly, pushing open a panelled door. 'Now, let's get you unpacked.'

Chapter 3

The room was large and light-coloured, with a single bed, an enormous wardrobe that had been built along the length of one wall, a pale wood dressing-table with a bowl of roses on it, two chairs and some bookshelves crammed with paperbacks and magazines.

I don't know why, somehow I'd been expecting to sleep in Sandie's room, and I was relieved and disappointed at the same time that I was actually going to be on my own. At least if I felt homesick, or wanted to cry, or just sit and be confused, I had the space to do it in. And someone in the Walker household, I realised gratefully, had already thought that through for me.

'Like the duvet?' Sandie balanced my case on its end in a chair and I wondered if the box of soap I'd brought for Mrs Walker would be all right. 'Mum and I went out and got it. We didn't really know your taste or anything, of course, but *I* think it's great!'

She smoothed down a corner of the bright red cover and grinned at me embarrassedly. 'It was the white hearts that really sold *me* on it. *Mum* wanted something all pale and embroidered to match the room. But you know what mums are like!'

'Yes!' I unzipped my small case and fumbled inside it. 'When you come to stay with me, *my* mama will probably have the entire room redecorated before you arrive!'

'*Mine* wanted to do that with this one!' Sandie giggled, collapsing across the bed. 'But when Dad told her she'd have to do it herself, she changed her mind pretty quickly. She's not very good with a paintbrush. What're you doing?'

I felt myself blush. My entire arm was trapped inside the case and I must've looked pretty stupid.

'I – I brought you presents.' My fingers closed round the package I knew was Sandie's and I sighed with relief. 'Here!' I flipped it towards her. 'Maybe you won't like them, but if not I'll take them home with me when I go and exchange them for something else.'

I turned away, still blushing, while she fumbled with the tissue wrapping-paper.

I'd brought some crystallised fruits for Mr Walker, because Mama and I hadn't known what else to get; the soap for Mrs Walker with the flamenco dancer on the front of the box; and a leather key-holder for Barry.

But Sandie's ear-rings were special. I'd seen them in the market when Mama and I had gone shopping, and I'd fallen in love with them.

'They're *beautiful*, Juanita!' She lay on her stomach holding them in her hands and staring down at them. 'Wow! Maggie'll eat her heart out over these! She's always going on about how she prefers unusual, *natural* things!' She held the ear-rings up and turned towards me. 'Will they suit me, d'you think?'

I looked at her. With her face still slightly swollen from the trip to the dentist and her curly hair all over the place, the ear-rings looked so *wrong* I couldn't help but giggle.

'What's the matter? I think they're wonderful!' She scrambled up, went over to the dressing-table and peered at herself in the small mirror. 'I mean, these little flowers and everything they have in them! Are they *real*?'

'Yes,' I nodded. 'Dried grasses, I think. Do you ever wear ear-rings?' I added hastily.

'I can't wear *these*!' she pulled a face. 'My ears aren't pierced!'

'Oh.' I felt an idiot. Mama had asked me about that when I'd bought them and I'd told her everybody had pierced ears these days. Everybody did have in Spain, and I'd thought London would be the same.

'Don't worry!' She bounded towards me and gave me an enormous hug. 'I'll get them done now! In fact, we'll make the appointment on Monday and you can come with me. I've always wanted to, but I've been too much of a coward in case it hurts a lot or gets infected.'

'Then they *will* be all right?' I knelt back on my heels and undid the big suitcase.

'They'll be terrific! Stop frowning! And just *wait* until you see Maggie's face when she notices them!'

'I have not,' I carefully pulled out the other gifts and put them together in a pile, 'brought anything for Maggie. I – I didn't know,' I trailed off, remembering the atmosphere downstairs.

'Why should you know? I never mentioned it in the letters,' Sandie shrugged. 'Anyway, if she and Barry have just split up again, she probably won't be around much. And *that*,' she added mysteriously, 'isn't going to please Mum! Never mind.' She smiled and punched me in the arm, which seemed to be her way of being friendly. 'It isn't our problem. We're going to have a *wonderful* summer, even if you *do* have to go to school through it, which is a bit yukky!'

'Yes.' I wanted to tell her I wasn't looking forward

to that, but she'd turned away again and was staring out of the window.

'Y'know,' she grunted while I unpacked my dresses and jeans, 'it's been terrific writing to you and now having you to stay and everything. But you're – well, *different* to the way I imagined! I thought you'd be tall and thin and sophisticated with raven-black hair and . . .'

'A rose in my teeth?' I laughed, hanging clothes up in the big wardrobe. Because there was nothing else in it they looked very lonely swinging from the rail.

'Not exactly! And you *do* have flashing eyes!' She looked at me seriously. 'But it's quite a relief to know you're more ordinary. Like me.'

'I thought the same thing, exactly!' I closed the louvred doors and pushed my empty case under the bed. 'I thought you'd be very pale and withdrawn and *English*. A perfect lady with a rose complexion!'

'More like a greenfly complexion!' She rubbed at her freckles furiously, then we stared at each other again and started to laugh.

'Me?' she choked. 'A *lady*! You wait until I tell Robin that one! Sometimes he doesn't even notice I'm a *girl*! Honestly, don't fellas make you sick?'

She grabbed me by the arm and I followed her while she showed me the bathroom and explained how to work the shower.

'Listen, my room's the one next to yours with "Do Not Disturb" on the door. Get yourself cleaned up and I'll wait for you there. We'd better not be too long otherwise Mum'll start creating. And Robin *did* say,' she leaned against the door frame wistfully, 'that he might look round tonight if his match finished early, so I'm going to go and change. I feel all tacky after that visit to his father. I *hate* dentists, don't you?'

It was the second question she'd asked me, but I suddenly realised she wasn't expecting any answer, so I just smiled and nodded, and after she'd disappeared, closed and locked the bathroom door behind me.

I scrubbed my hands and neck, splashed warm water on my face and looked at myself in the mirror.

My hair *was* black, and it was also a mess because Papa wanted me to wear it long and I kept cheating and cutting bits off with my nail scissors.

I wasn't tall. In fact, I was slightly shorter than Sandie, and I needed to lose weight, but at home Mama and Papa wouldn't even *listen* to me when I talked about going on a diet. They said it was all just puppy-fat and in another two or three years I'd be able to tell what my natural shape was going to be. The trouble was I couldn't seem to convince them I didn't want to *wait* another two or three years! I wanted to be perfect now.

I wanted to have a figure like Maggie's with legs that went on for ever, so that people like Barry would look at me and smile and squeeze my hand, the way he'd done with hers before they had their argument.

'Fat chance!' I'd heard someone say that in a film once. 'No way, Juanita! Even if your eyes *do* flash!'

I peered at them, wondering what Sandie meant. To me they were just the eyes I looked out from every day. Maybe they did smile and frown, and even flash, but I never *saw* that because I was always behind them.

'Come on, Juanita!' Sandie suddenly pounded at the door. 'What's the matter? Fallen down the plughole? Haven't you heard Mum yelling? Supper's ready and we're all having a drink in the garden!'

'I'll be right out!' I left the spot I'd just noticed alone, ran away the water from the basin and dried myself off.

'See you in a minute then. Okay? Robin's turned up and I want to show him my ear-rings!'

'Okay.' I unbolted the door and went back to my room, then changed quickly into the one short dress that hadn't creased like all the others and padded downstairs barefoot.

I found my way into the kitchen easily enough, and I'd just worked out that if I went through the open door at the far end I'd probably be with the others in the garden, when Barry walked in and stopped dead, smiling at me with surprise.

'We-e-ell!' He let out a whistle. 'And how does everybody suppose I'm going to contain myself all summer with you walking around like *that*?'

'Pardon?' I glanced down at my bare legs. 'I'm sorry. I don't understand. Have I done something wrong?'

'Not in the slightest!' He opened the fridge and pulled out some more cans of beer. 'You're just likely to cause a couple of earthquakes in the immediate neighbourhood, that's all, and young Robin may have a premature heart attack!'

'The dress? It's not suitable?' I felt tongue-tied and anxious. It was an old white sundress with a scoop neck that I wore on the beach at home because it was cool and comfortable.

'The dress is fine, Juanita. Very charming. Barry's taking the mickey out of you. Making a joke,' Mr Walker explained, smiling at me.

'Oh!' I smiled back gratefully. 'Then I am not

in bad taste? I have not done something socially unacceptable?' It was the only way I could think of putting it, but even to my ears the words sounded peculiar and stilted.

'Your taste's absolutely fine by me! You look terrific!' Barry slung his arm round my shoulders casually and grinned down at me. I swallowed hard, because I was suddenly having difficulty breathing. 'Now come on out and drink some fizzy wine to celebrate me finding you safely at Heathrow! Robin's turned up at last and Sandie's doing her adoring puppy bit!'

I went with him in a slight daze, very conscious of the way his bare arm felt against my bare shoulders, and I was relieved when Mrs Walker beckoned me forward and offered me a glass of wine.

'All right?' she smiled.

'Yes.' But I felt terribly shy and embarrassed, and I was glad Barry had wandered off to talk to his father. 'Where's Sandie?'

'We're here!' She suddenly bounced out through open French windows. 'I was turning on the stereo so we could have some background music because Mum's made salad and we're eating out here.

'Juanita,' she grinned at me proudly, 'this is Robin Derwent. Robin – this is my pen-friend. The one I told you about.'

For absolutely no reason, when Robin shook my hand, I started to blush again.

He was a couple of years younger than Barry, but almost as tall, and the look on his face as he stood there smiling at me reminded me very vividly of the soppy slobbering look Elvira had given me when I'd offered her a crisp in the kitchen.

'Isn't he *gorgeous*?' Sandie whispered as she topped up her own drink. 'Don't you think he's quite the loveliest thing on two legs you've ever seen?'

'We-ell,' I didn't want to hurt her feelings, 'he seems very nice. Have you known him for a long time?'

'Years!' She waved her arm dramatically at the garden and Elvira woofed sleepily. 'Practically ever since I was born. We even went to the same infant school. But I've only just *noticed* him, if you know what I mean, in the last year. The trouble is,' she added gloomily as we went into the kitchen to collect plates of food for everybody, 'I don't think *he's* noticed me. Not properly, anyway. Not the way,' she sniffed slightly and I wondered if she was trying not to cry, 'he *certainly* noticed you just now!.

'Juanita,' she picked a lettuce leaf out of a poly-thene bag and nibbled it thoughtfully, 'you're not going to be a *problem* to me this summer, are you?'

'Problem?' I frowned. I had no idea what she was getting at.

'Well, you're a stranger here and everything, and you *are* Spanish, and you do have wonderful eyes and,' she glanced at me quickly, 'pretty nice legs. Particularly in that outfit! So you're not, well, going to get in my way or anything, are you?'

'Oh Sandie!' I suddenly realised she was as insecure as I was, and I wanted to hug her. 'D'you mean am I going to try to take Robin away from you?'

She swallowed the last of the lettuce, wiped her hands on the seat of her white jeans and nodded without looking at me.

I sat down.

I'd only been in England a couple of hours, and it

30

didn't exactly feel like enough time to tell Sandie I didn't fancy Robin Derwent in the slightest!

But Barry?

Well *that* was an entirely different story!

Chapter 4

Fortunately Sandie couldn't ask me why I'd gone quiet because Mrs Walker bustled into the kitchen wanting to know why we were taking so long with everything, and as I helped her with the salad bowls and meat platters, Sandie slipped back into the garden.

'Love's young nightmare!' Barry laughed, noticing me watching Sandie and Robin talking by the back gate. 'I'm afraid the little sister is having a bad attack! What about you, Juanita?' He took the basket of garlic bread from me and put it on the wooden table. 'Is there some dashing young Spaniard eating his heart out for you at home?'

'N-no.' I took the fork Mr Walker was offering me and tried to smile. 'My parents are strict. I may have boys who are friends. But boyfriends . . .?' I shrugged. 'Papa would shout a lot, I think!'

'*I* shout a lot!' Mr Walker smiled. 'But it never seems to make a great deal of difference. They come and they go and I'm accused of not remembering that the one with the spiky red hair and a safety-pin through his ear isn't Jim but Tony!'

'To be perfectly honest, they all look exactly alike. Robin's the only one who's instantly recognisable, isn't he, dear?' He filled up his wife's glass and turned to her, still smiling.

'At least Robin and Sandie aren't a problem!' Mrs Walker murmured, but although she was trying to laugh, the words sounded cold . . . and sad too.

'*Yet*!' Mr Walker laughed, too, and threw his wife something that seemed like a warning message.

'Come off it, Dad!' Barry finished his beer and wiped his mouth with the back of his hand. 'You know Sandie and I are what keep you and Mum young! Without us, what else would you have to worry about?'

'Just a few minor things like the mortgage and the telephone bills. Nothing important!' Mr Walker picked up a chicken drumstick and gnawed it. 'And talking about telephones, have you . . .?'

'No.' Barry's face darkened and I busied myself with a dish of coleslaw. 'And I'm not going to. What's the point? We've been over and over it, so why don't we just let it die a natural death?'

'You know perfectly well why not!' His mother suddenly rounded on him. 'You're talking about going to France on a university exchange for final year. Well, academically that may be the best thing for you. But what about Maggie?'

'Mum,' I moved uneasily away from the family group as he started to talk, 'Maggie knows the answers just as well as you or I do,' I heard him say. 'But it doesn't seem to make any difference. I've done everything I can, but this afternoon she was so rude and self-centred I just gave up.

'Anyway,' I felt him glance in my direction and I

studied my salad carefully, wishing Sandie would give up cooing at Robin and come back and join me, 'we're really not being fair to Juanita with all this silly squabbling, are we?'

I looked towards him through my eyelashes, hoping it wasn't too obvious I'd been listening. He was smiling at his mother – a very warm, almost pleading smile, and quite suddenly Mrs Walker seemed to relax.

'You're absolutely right!' She patted him affectionately on the shoulder. 'Maggie's not the only person who's been rude. I'm sorry, Juanita.'

She came over and perched beside me. 'This must all seem very bad-mannered and off-hand of us. But it's nothing to worry about, and it's high time we started talking about you, instead.'

I didn't want to talk about me in the slightest. I knew all about me and my life and it was pretty boring.

I wanted to know more about the Walkers and Maggie and whether Elvira had tickly paws and if Tiddlykins ever came into the house or not, instead. But for ages I heard myself explaining how my Spanish summers were usually spent with Dolores and Katerine on the beach; how Papa had been furious with my language results at school, which was one of the reasons he'd allowed me to come to London, so I'd improve, and how he wanted me to be a teacher when I didn't know *what* I wanted to be yet.

It was almost ten o'clock when Mr Walker brought the tray of coffee mugs out into the garden. Mrs Walker was doing the other dishes and Robin had disappeared ages before, muttering something to me about seeing me tomorrow for the roast beef. I'd smiled and tried to stay as far away from him as possible. Something warned me that *I* wasn't going to be the problem for Sandie this summer, but the way Robin seemed to consider himself God's gift to girls could very well be.

Barry had gone round to see some friends, although Sandie whispered to me that he was just trying to escape his mother and any more questions.

'If she'd leave them *both* alone,' she groaned, holding her stomach and complaining she'd eaten too many strawberries, 'everything would probably be perfectly all right. Why do mothers always have to interfere and think they know best when sometimes they don't at all?'

'I don't know.' I stretched out on the sun-lounger feeling suddenly very sleepy and confused. It was almost dark, but the sky had a reflected red glow to it from all the street lights, and mosquitoes and gnats buzzed under the trees. 'Perhaps we'll be the same when we're mothers?'

'I'm not sure I *want* to be one! It seems like too much hassle all the time! And I'm not sure I want to get married, either. I'd rather just have a string of lovers, starting with Robin of course,' she murmured wistfully, then got up quickly and rubbed her bare arms. 'Brr! Time we went in! Somebody's just walked over my grave!'

'*Qué?*' I didn't understand.

'It's just an expression meaning I've got goose-bumps!'

'Goose's bumps?' My head was beginning to reel again. 'Where are the geese?'

'Oh Juanita, honestly!' She pulled me to my feet

and punched me lightly. 'It means pimples! Look. You've got them as well! It's getting cold! It's nothing to *do* with geese!

'Anyway,' she picked up our empty mugs and I followed her towards the house, 'there's a film I want to watch on telly. What about you?'

'Me?' I glanced at my watch. It was still on Spanish time, which meant my head and body were convinced it was almost half-past eleven. 'If you don't mind, I think I'll go to bed. I'm tired.'

'Of course you are.' Mrs Walker took the plates I was carrying and dumped them in the sink. 'But d'you want to ring your parents to let them know you've arrived safely?'

I thought about that for a moment, then shook my head, hoping nobody would notice how my lip had just started to tremble.

I knew if I spoke to Papa – or, worse, if Mama answered the phone – I'd probably simply burst into tears. As Sandie had said about something else earlier, it would finish me off, and I didn't want that to happen.

I wanted them, and the Walkers, to be proud and think I was grown-up and perfectly capable of coping in a foreign country by myself.

'You're sure?' Mrs Walker looked at me so closely I had to turn away and pretend to pat Elvira.

'Tomorrow,' I murmured. 'It is very late.'

Sandie waved at me as I passed the living-room and Mr Walker shouted out for me to sleep well, but as I got undressed in the pale-coloured room upstairs, I had a funny feeling that sleep might take a very long time to come.

Chapter 5

In fact it didn't, although I did wake up a couple of times during the night half-wondering where I was and convinced I could hear loud voices.

I lay, watching the unfamiliar shadows on the walls and listening to a cat that might've been Tiddlykins yelling plaintively in the distance.

Then everywhere, including my mind, must've gone quiet, and when I woke next it was because I could feel a terrible weight on my chest and I seemed to be having difficulty breathing.

I opened one eye.

Elvira licked my nose and a big fluffy paw scraped at my shoulder.

Sandie laughed.

'She's telling you it's time to get up and take her out! She obviously thinks you're one of the family now!'

Sandie perched on the side of the bed and nodded towards the small table. 'I brought you a coffee, though Mum says you can have breakfast and everything when you want it. Did you sleep okay?'

'Mmm.' I pushed Elvira to one side and struggled up on my pillows, rubbing my eyes. 'What time is it?'

'Half-ten. I've been on the go for *hours*! But Mum said we should let you lie in because you were bound to be tired. Incidentally, it's raining, which means it'll be dead boring going out, but at least Robin can't play cricket!' She rubbed her thighs gleefully and I caught myself wondering why I didn't feel as relieved as she obviously did by that prospect.

But what was left of the morning went past in such a whirl that I didn't really have time to think any more at all.

Although I said I wasn't very hungry, Mrs Walker insisted on making me a cooked breakfast with bacon and eggs and sausages. I couldn't finish it all, but when nobody was looking Elvira helped me with one of the sausages and some toast!

I rang my parents, but they'd gone out, and somehow that made me feel much more alone than I had before.

'For goodness sake, Sandie!' Mrs Walker was shouting in exasperation just as I walked back into the kitchen. 'Stop interfering with the lunch! If you put any more hundreds-and-thousands on that trifle Bob Derwent'll have to have an emergency session for us all at his surgery this afternoon!'

Sandie stuck her tongue out at her mum's back and I smothered a giggle, imagining us all being lined up for the dentist's chair.

'Well,' she scattered the remainder of her handful of little coloured sugar balls all over the whipped cream, 'what d'you want me to do instead, then?'

'Go and play on a busy crossing?' Barry walked into the kitchen, his face and hair glistening with rain, and I started having another peculiar breathless feeling that had nothing to do with Elvira lying on me.

'I've got a better idea!' Mr Walker looked up from the table where he'd been reading the papers. 'Why don't you and Juanita take the dog for a walk on the common? You can feed her to the ducks or something!'

Elvira barked and wagged her tail, as if she knew

we were talking about her, then she noticed something beyond the open back door, gave a tremendous bound forward, and for the next five minutes we all chased her round the garden trying to stop *her* chasing a pale grey fluffy cat that had been quite happily digging a hole in a flower-bed.

When Sandie and I finally came back from trying to exhaust Elvira by throwing sticks for her on the common, I hurried upstairs to have a shower and change. Somehow Elvira seemed to think I was her own personal doormat, and my jeans were covered in hair and muddy paw-prints!

The rest of the afternoon was a blur of meeting the Derwents, eating far too much English food, and trying – while Sandie and Mrs Walker were making coffee – to avoid getting too close to Robin.

I simply didn't trust him one inch. He was too good-looking – and he knew it! I was pretty positive, too, that behind Sandie's back he flirted with every other girl he met, and I'd absolutely no intentions of letting him get away with that with me!

'It's a shame,' he almost purred, breathing at me so deeply that his shirt fell open across his chest to show his suntan, 'you start language school on Tuesday. Still, you'll be in the West End, won't you? Perhaps I can take you to lunch one day? I know quite a few neat places in Soho.'

'I – I'm not sure that will be at all possible,' I stammered formally, moving away from him. After he'd left the Walkers' the previous evening he must've eaten a lot of garlic and onions somewhere because his breath reeked! 'I don't know my schedule, you see, and there are trips I understand I have to make, to improve my English knowledge.'

'I can think of *lots* of ways of improving that!' he leered, brushing his arm against mine – just as Sandie came into the room and saw us standing together.

'I don't think so!' I looked him straight in the eye. Sandie was my friend. I was her guest. Even if I'd thought he was attractive, because she cared about him there was no way I would've encouraged Robin Derwent!

I made a feeble-sounding excuse about wanting to try to contact my parents again and hurried out of the room, feeling rather like the weather – overcast, grey and miserable!

'Cheer up, little J!' Barry clapped me on the shoulder as I sat down beside the telephone in the hall. 'What's wrong? Mum's Yorkshires sitting too heavily on the old tum?'

'*Qué?*' I frowned. Apart from anything else, I thought he'd gone out directly after lunch.

'You look unhappy.' He settled himself on the bottom step of the stairs and frowned at me. 'Homesick?'

'No. Yes. I'm not sure.' I shook my head. 'It's all,' I shrugged, not certain how to find the proper words, 'different and . . .'

'Strange?'

'Yes.' I stared down at the leather telephone pad. He was too close, and I found that closeness very disturbing. 'I am a foreigner. I don't know your ways.' I raised my eyebrows and made myself look at him.

'Robin Derwent was coming on a bit strong, is that it?' Barry's voice was gentle, and I swallowed hard then nodded.

'He is,' I tried to explain, 'Sandie's. He has not the right to — to come on so strong, as you put it, with me. She will be hurt and I will not be able to tell her it is not my fault.'

'She'll be hurt anyway. It's running in this family at the moment!' Barry said bitterly. 'But I'll have a word with Robin, if you like, and tell him to lay off.'

'N-no.' I took a deep breath. 'These are my battles. I'll fight them in my own way. But perhaps, if you could explain to Sandie?' I glanced at her brother. 'Tell her I'm not interested? This might make a difference.'

'I'll try. But I'm only her brother.' He pulled himself to his feet, leaned across and put his hand under my chin, lifting it so I had to look him straight in the eyes. 'Just make very sure *you* don't get hurt this summer, too. In other words,' he smiled, and I felt my heart gulp, 'don't take any of us too seriously.'

It was a warning. I knew it was a warning, and I knew instinctively that Barry had worked out how confused I felt about *him*.

I nodded slowly, lowering my eyes and trying very hard to ignore the fact that all I could properly see were the blond hairs on the back of his brown hands.

'Good.' He let my chin go. 'The thing about summers is that they're fine while they're here and happening, but autumn always comes and usually that changes everything.

'Now why don't you go and have a quick wash? It might freshen you up. You can ring your folks later. I'll go and explain to everybody you can't get through or something. That'll give you a few minutes' grace at least.'

I looked at him again, struggling with all the

breathlessness inside me.

'Thank you,' I said very quietly. 'You're a nice person.'

'I know.' He was smiling, but his face was far-away and sad. 'I'm absolutely *wonderful*! I never make mistakes, or get myself into something I don't know how to get out of or cope with! Pity the rest of the world doesn't have your kind of insight, Juanita!'

I wanted to reach across and touch him. I wanted to ask him if I could help him in any way, maybe just by listening to him if he wanted to talk. I wanted to say that, although I was a foreigner, I was still a human person, exactly like him, and that although I might not fully understand the unhappinesses and tensions, telling them aloud might help.

We stood looking at each other for one of those moments that feel as if they're stretching on for ever.

He was twenty. He was at college, and experienced. He drove a car and joked with his mother, and his sister called him 'nearly a genius'.

I was sixteen. Overweight. Inexperienced. Spanish.

I didn't know very much about anything. I was shy and clumsy. My English was chaotic – and I'd never been properly in love. How could I expect someone like Barry to take me as anything more serious than Sandie's pen-friend and a member of the family for the next six weeks?

Suddenly I wanted to rush away and hide in the pale room upstairs.

I wanted to pull the red cover with its white hearts over my head and not come out from under it until it was time for my plane to take me back home!

I wanted to curl up inside myself until the chrysalis that was me at the moment eventually cracked open, and the butterfly that would be me tomorrow struggled out into the air. *Then* I'd be able to unfold my wings in the sunshine and have Barry look at me the way I *wanted* him to look at me.

But before I could say or do anything, a key turned in the front door lock, Elvira – who'd come out and lain down at my feet – growled softly. The door opened.

And Maggie stood there.

Chapter 6

Barry's eyebrows lifted in surprise when he saw her, but before either of them could say anything I excused myself and ran upstairs.

Logically I knew I was over-reacting. There was no reason *why* Maggie shouldn't have a key – except that it made her even more special then I'd imagined. But if she and Barry had had their final row, perhaps she was only coming to return it.

I stomped across my room to the window and looked out. Rain was trickling down the glass and it suddenly seemed as if the sky was crying.

My head ached. My mouth felt dry and gritty, and I sat down on the bed feeling very small and insignificant.

I'd promised Mama I wouldn't do anything stupid like fall in love over the summer, and certainly not with an English guy.

'Don't be silly!' We'd been in the kitchen at home and I'd been stoning olives for her special paella. 'English boys will all laugh at me because I'm not sophisticated and trendy and punk! And I wouldn't know how to talk to them anyway. I'm bad enough with Spanish boys!'

'Sometimes,' she'd glanced up from slicing garlic, 'you don't have to *talk*, Juanita. And that's what worries me most. I read the English papers and magazines when Fernanda does my hair. English boys,' she'd hesitated, then swirled the mussels round in their bowl so their shells crashed against each other, 'seem much more *knowing* than our boys.

'It may be,' she'd been embarrassed and I'd had difficulty not giggling as she'd struggled for words, 'one could kiss you. A kiss can be of no importance, or of all importance. But what continues after . . .'

She'd trailed off and I'd tried to reassure her I wasn't planning on kissing *anybody*, let alone allowing anything else to happen. And because she was my mama I think she'd believed me.

But now, I pleated the duvet cover between my fingers so the white hearts all ran into each other, less than twenty-four hours after I'd arrived I wanted to forget about those reassurances.

I stretched out, closed my eyes and stroked my right shoulder with my left hand, imagining it was Barry doing that.

I wanted *him* to kiss me.

More than anything else in the world, I wanted him to kiss me!

I could imagine how it would feel. I could imagine how he would look; how his eyes would slightly mist over; how his hand with the blond hairs on its back would gently tilt my chin up, the way he'd done earlier. How . . .

'What's wrong with you?' The bed shook as Sandie threw herself across the end of it. 'Aren't you feeling well?'

'I – I'm okay.' I struggled to smile and sit up. 'I had a bit of a headache, that's all. I'm sorry. I'm being very rude.'

'Don't be daft!' She bounced to her feet and twirled round. 'But if you think you can make it, grab a coat. Robin's suggested we go back to his place and watch a couple of videos. He's ringing some people we know, and we'll have a sort of party to introduce you to everybody.

'Mum's agreed. She thinks it's a great idea, and Mr and Mrs Derwent are staying here, so we won't have to be on our best behaviour or anything!'

The last thing I wanted was to go to any kind of party, particularly one involving Robin Derwent, but I couldn't think of a sensible way to refuse so I dragged myself through to the bathroom, washed my face, smeared on a little make-up and joined Sandie downstairs.

Nobody mentioned Maggie or Barry. The two sets of parents simply smiled and patted us and sent us off to enjoy ourselves as if we were children going to kindergarten. Sometimes I think parents don't realise their children aren't children any more.

In fact, it wasn't quite as bad as I'd imagined.

The others who turned up seemed quite nice, although none of them spoke to me very much, and when they did they said everything too loudly and too slowly, as if I were deaf and had to lip-read.

I've done the same thing myself with foreigners

who don't speak much Spanish. But it made me feel very isolated.

I kept out of Robin's way as much as possible. Fortunately Sandie was so happy to have him on her own without older people around that she spent most of the evening hugging and kissing him, which I found embarrassing but which everybody else seemed to assume was normal.

One girl called Bev *did* try to talk to me. She was very tall, very thin and very serious, with masses of red hair, a CND badge and heavy-framed spectacles that made her eyes look enormous.

She wanted to know all about the economic and political situation in Spain, and when I told her I didn't really know much about that at all, she sniffed.

'Don't you realise,' she said, jamming her spectacles more firmly on to her nose, 'that all the European countries ought to *help* each other? That what we need is a united peace policy for the world? Now where does Spain stand regarding that?'

'Leave Juanita alone! This isn't the United Nations!' a voice laughed, and I looked up, relieved at the interruption. 'She's here on *holiday*, Bev!'

'That doesn't mean she's not *aware*, Joe!' She tossed that amazing hair at him, then got to her feet and almost growled, 'I'll talk with you about this again, Juanita, when that *idiot* isn't around!'

'Thanks!' I sipped the last of my wine and smiled at the boy who'd squatted down beside me on the floor. 'I'm sorry, but I really *don't* know much about these things!'

'Don't worry.' He passed me a bowl of crisps. 'And don't take Bev too seriously, either. She's only been like this since she got into the debating society at school. She's a good laugh when you get to know her. A lot better than most of this mob,' he indicated the other couples sprawled round the room.

'I'm Joe Berry, by the way. I live just up the street from Sandie, so we're neighbours.'

'Oh.' I smiled. He was good-looking in an almost Spanish way. Dark-haired and dark-eyed with a wide smile that made me think of Barry. 'So you know the family well, then?'

'Yup! Barry and I sometimes play football together, when Maggie hasn't got him running all over London for her, that is! She was round this afternoon, wasn't she? I saw her go in the gate. I thought it was all finished again?'

I shook my head, not knowing what to say, but there was something about him – *and* the way he stayed beside me when Robin Derwent oiled his way over, all teeth and open shirt – that convinced me he'd be a friend if I needed one.

'Sandie has to go home,' Robin purred, touching me on the arm for far longer than necessary. 'She's had a *wee* bit too much wine, if you see what I mean?'

I looked at the sofa.

Sandie was slumped against the cushions with a stupid grin on her face, waggling her fingers at me. Her lipstick, or what was left of it, was smeared, her sweatshirt was rucked up at the waist and her hair was all over the place.

'I – I'll take her, then, shall I?' I asked, thankful for the chance to get away. I've had wine with meals since I was small and never been drunk, which was more than you could say for anybody else other than Joe in the rest of the room!

'Well, I can't really leave. Though I'd *much* rather be alone with you!' Robin breathed all over me, smelling like a day-old dirty ashtray from the cigarettes he'd been smoking.

'Come on, Juanita!' Joe turned and headed towards Sandie. 'I've got to go anyway. I'm working tomorrow. I'll give you a hand with her. After all, Robin,' he looked at him and raised a sarcastic eyebrow, 'we all know how much you care about her!'

The damp cool night air felt fresh after the mugginess of the party, and I gulped in lungfuls of it while Joe more or less carried Sandie down the steps to the street.

I followed slowly.

There was something about the careful way he was holding her and treating her that made me think he was much fonder of her than he ever said to anybody, and I suddenly caught myself wondering if everybody in England was as complicated as the members of the Walker family!

Chapter 7

Fortunately I managed to get Sandie into bed without her parents seeing her.

I had a feeling they'd be none too pleased at the state she was in, and the next morning when Mr Walker started asking me questions about how I'd enjoyed my evening I just smiled and nodded and let him think I didn't understand as much English as I was *beginning* to understand.

It seemed to me that being able to play the part of the dumb foreigner might have its advantages after all!

Sandie wasn't even up when we left for the West End to enrol me officially at the language school, and after a bewildering morning filling in forms and trying to understand the schedule that was laid out, I felt exhausted.

The other students in my class varied from a married Japanese couple in their early twenties to a German boy my own age who was so shy he blushed whenever anyone spoke to him.

Miss Ellen, the teacher, seemed pleasant. She was youngish, too, and told us she'd been an actress before she trained as a language teacher.

'The schedule for visits to famous places and other parts of the country isn't a rigid one. You don't have to go on any of these trips if you'd prefer not to. Take the lists back to your student accommodation and read them carefully, then mark off any that interest you.

'The weekend in the Lake District and Scotland should be fun.' She beamed encouragingly at us all. 'And some of the days out are good value, too. But if, as in your case Juanita,' she turned and looked at me, which made me go as pink as the German boy had been going, 'you're already staying with an English family, you may not want to bother with these extra activities.'

There was a bit more chat. We met some other teachers and some of the more advanced students on other courses, then our class was dismissed and we were free to do whatever we liked.

The Japanese couple wanted to go shopping.

Two girls from Italy, who were very serious and reminded me of Bev from last night's party, were planning on finding the British Museum, and Dieter asked me stumblingly if I'd like to see round Covent Garden with him, but I shook my head.

'I have to go back,' I explained gently. 'The girl I'm staying with, my pen-friend, is having her ears pierced today and she wants me to be with her.'

But when I finally walked into the kitchen of the Walkers' home, feeling hot and bothered and flustered after almost getting lost changing trains at Victoria, it was perfectly obvious that Sandie didn't want to go *anywhere*.

In fact, she didn't even seem to want to talk to me.

She was sitting in a chair with a cup of cold, greasy-looking coffee in front of her and a very peculiar expression on her face.

'Hi!' I grinned, dumping my bag and books on the table and sprawling into the other chair. Stupidly, because I'd wanted to make a good impression and hadn't realised how far you have to walk to get anywhere in central London, I'd worn shoes with high heels, and my feet hurt.

'Hello.' She turned away and stared through the window.

'How are you feeling?' It was hot and sultry again outside, but the temperature in the kitchen had dropped by several degrees since I'd sat down.

'All right.' She frowned at something in the garden, and I looked at her closely, suddenly realising she must've been crying.

'It was a good party,' I tried tentatively. 'I enjoyed myself very much. Your friends are nice.'

'Yes. Aren't they?' Flat, unemotional, uninterested *nothing*.

Obviously I was at fault somewhere, but *where* I couldn't imagine, so I got up, crossed over to the fridge and opened the door. Mrs Walker had told me to help myself to anything I wanted, and although I didn't really *want* anything, I desperately needed something to do. I couldn't just sit there with a stupid smile on my face waiting for Sandie to tell me what was wrong.

'The school seems nice, too,' I murmured, levering the ring-pull off a can of Diet-Pepsi. 'The teacher's funny.'

'Wonderful!' Sandie started drumming her nails against the tabletop. 'Tall, dark and handsome like Robin, is he?'

'No.' I frowned at my drink. 'She's small, fair, square-shaped and engaged to one of the other teachers. What's Robin got to do with this, anyway?'

'As if you didn't *know*!' She got to her feet so quickly the chair rattled against the table and over-balanced with a crash. 'Stop acting the innocent!

'You've only been here a couple of days, which means,' she laughed spitefully, 'you'll be leaving in precisely 42 days and 9 hours! I know. I've counted them! And I can't *wait*!'

'Sandie,' I was going hot and cold and my stomach felt peculiar, as if I might suddenly have to dash to the loo, 'please, I don't understand! What's wrong? Why are you so unfriendly?'

'Why shouldn't I be?' She flounced across the kitchen and wrenched open the door. 'I thought you were my *friend*! Your letters were always friendly enough!' Then without a backward glance she banged out into the hall and I heard her footsteps running upstairs.

I stayed where I was. I didn't know what else *to* do. Then after her bedroom door slammed, I wandered miserably into the garden and sat down beside Elvira, who gave me a paw and whimpered at me as if she wasn't having a very good day, either.

'What *have* I done?' I blinked back tears and muttered to myself. 'Why is she like this? Who do I talk to?'

Elvira sat up and licked my face sympathetically.

'I don't want her Robin!' I hugged the big fluffy animal, glad to have something warm and alive close to me. 'I don't even *like* him. And I don't trust him! So why?'

'Why what?' A shadow fell across the grass in front of me and Elvira woofed a welcome. 'What's up? First day at school getting you down?'

Barry squatted beside me and brushed my hair away from my face.

'Hey! You're crying! What *has* happened, Juanita?'

'Nothing! I don't know!' Because he was there I suddenly clung to him and buried my face in his shirt. 'I'm sorry, Barry. I'm your guest. I should be cheerful and helpful. Mama made me promise I would be. But Sandie,' I gulped and sniffed, 'was very nasty when I got in. I've offended her in some way, but I don't understand how!'

'Oh, is *that* all!' He pushed me away from him a little and sat back on his heels, grinning in relief. 'I thought for a minute you'd been mugged on the tube, or got enrolled at the wrong school or something serious!'

'*All*!' I exploded, spraying tears everwhere.

All! Surely the things Sandie had said about me leaving in 42 days and 9 hours were more than enough? Nobody, not even my worst enemy at home, had ever talked to me like that before!

'Yes.' Barry got up, went into the kitchen and came back with some kitchen paper for me to blow my nose on. '*All*!

'Apart from having a hangover, which she certainly has though she's been denying it to Mum most of the morning, my dear little sister is in a thoroughly evil frame of mind because of Robin Derwent! Come on!' He held out his hand, grabbed mine and pulled me to my feet. 'I'll show you!

'Mum, who is a lovely lady but a bit thick some-times,' he explained as we walked towards the open French windows, 'thinks this is a truly *wonnerful*,' he drawled the word sarcastically, 'gesture of Robin's. Sandie thinks he's a heel. And *I* think he's a lot worse than a creep! But you make up your own mind!'

He stood to one side and nodded for me to go past him into the lounge.

I blinked in the dim light, trying to bring things into focus and make sense of what Barry was saying.

Then I gasped.

On a low coffee table in the centre of the room was a white pottery vase with a dozen long-stemmed red roses in it.

'Robin sent Sandie *these*?' I looked sideways at Barry, but his mouth tightened and he shook his head.

'Wrong. Take a closer look. Read the card.'

I frowned, understanding everything even less than

I had before.

'They arrived after you'd gone, which is probably just as well in the interests of world peace!' Barry grunted, striding to the table and lifting up a small white envelope which he handed to me. 'Naturally Sandie *did* think they might be for her!'

I opened the white envelope shakily and read the neat lettering. It was typical of Robin Derwent that he'd written it in gold ink.

'I DON'T KNOW ANYTHING ABOUT SPANISH FLORA AND FAUNA,' it said. 'I ONLY KNOW THE LOVELIEST FLOWER HAS JUST WALKED INTO MY LIFE ROBIN D.'

Chapter 8

I felt physically sick and I looked at Barry helplessly.

'This,' I tapped the card with the envelope, 'is nonsense! Stupid! I find him unpleasant! So why . . .?'

'Because you're a new face, I guess. Because he imagines every girl in the world is throwing herself at him, and probably because you *haven't* he's decided he'd better make you, pretty damn soon!'

'Then he is in for – how d'you say it? One big surprise!' I almost spat the words and Barry glanced at me in amusement. 'Please, give me his address now! I wish to throw something at him, but it is not myself!'

I scooped the roses out of the vase, stamped through to the kitchen and tore some more kitchen roll off the holder to wrap round the stems.

'Come on, Elvira!' I took her lead down from the hook by the door. 'We have a call to make and I might need protection!'

Barry didn't say anything, but he scrawled Robin's address across the front of the small white envelope and gave it to me. As I marched down the street with the dog beside me I inwardly prayed Robin Derwent wouldn't be at home.

If he was, I was quite likely to hit him over the head with the thorny part of his roses, then pull the petals off the poor flowers themselves, and stuff them into his mouth one by one until he suffocated!

I didn't care if they locked me up in an English prison for ever! It was the very *least* I could do for Sandie!

Mrs Derwent answered my third ring at the doorbell and raised her eyebrows in surprise when I pushed the bunch of flowers at her.

'Would you tell your *son*,' I emphasised the word as heavily as I could, 'that his unwelcome gift has been received and is here returned! Would you also please tell him,' even Elvira was taken aback, 'that if he as much as *talks* to me over the next 42 days and,' I glanced at my watch, 'eight and one-quarter hours, I will telephone your wonderful London policemen and inform them he is pestering me!'

I wouldn't, and I knew I wouldn't, but I had to say something!

'He is a creep!' I added over my shoulder as Elvira towed me down the path.

I slammed the wrought-iron gate behind me and stamped back the way I'd come.

Barry was eating a sandwich in the kitchen when

we came in and he raised both eyebrows at me.

'Well? Do we have to bail you out for murder, or just for grievous bodily harm?' he asked lightly.

I hung Elvira's lead back on its hook and sat down, feeling very tired and very weak. Normally I never get angry, and never in my life had I been *so* angry!

'Is Sandie still upstairs?' I looked at Barry, but he shook his head.

'Joe Berry came round to see if you both wanted to play tennis. I told Sandie *you* seemed a bit upset. *She* said that served you right and shot off with him!

'Don't worry, Juanita.' He crammed the rest of the sandwich into his mouth and got to his feet. 'Give it another hour and whatever you've done to Robin'll be all over the district! Then no doubt Sandie,' he grinned tiredly, 'will rush around his hurt feelings like a ministering angel. But in the long run she'll calm down and you'll be friends again!

'Now if you're sure you're okay, I must dash. Mum should be back soon, and if there's anything you want just keep on opening cupboards until you find it. But if any skeletons fall out, kick them to one side. Okay?'

He gave my shoulder a quick squeeze as he brushed past me, and I looked at him gratefully, a lot of other different, even more confusing, thoughts tumbling into my head again.

'Okay?' he repeated, hesitating in the doorway as if there was something else he wanted to add.

'Fine.' The anger had completely disappeared, and I simply felt numb and lonely.

Chapter 9

After Barry left I took the books and papers the school had given me out into the garden and tried to study them.

In a fit of rebellion I put ticks against every day-trip and outing, including the Scottish visit, I could find. At least these would mean I needn't be around the Walker household more than absolutely necessary.

But then, as the late afternoon sun began to warm through me and the enormous furry bumblebees buzzed in the flower-beds, I began to relax.

'Bumblebees shouldn't be able to fly, you know, Elvira,' I scratched the top of the dog's head sleepily and she panted a smile at me. 'Aeronautically speaking, if you can speak in such a silly way,' I giggled, 'the moment they take off, they should crash!'

'Shouldn't we all?' The unfamiliar voice made me blink and I struggled to sit up in the sun-lounger. 'Isn't anybody else at home? Have they *actually* decided you don't need a babysitter any more?'

Maggie, wearing not a great deal of anything very much, stood in front of me with a worried little pout on her face.

'Well?' She sank gracefully on to the grass, her legs folding around her in elegant V-curves. 'Where's Barry?'

'He – he had to go out,' I stuttered. 'He didn't say where. Sandie is playing tennis and Mrs Walker should be back soon,' I added limply, as if any of that mattered.

'Oh.' She pulled a daisy and started picking the petals off it. For some reason I suddenly realised she was as nervous of me as I was of her and I wondered why. 'Did Barry take the car? Or don't you know that, either?'

'I'm sorry.' I shook my head. 'He was eating a sandwich when I came in. Then he left. He was helpful to me earlier and he stayed to make sure I was all right, I think,' I added thoughtfully, because that *was* what he must've done.

'I'll bet! He thinks his middle name's Sir Galahad! Sometimes even *I* think it is, too.' The daisy was almost naked and her tight scarlet shorts were covered in white petals. She brushed them away impatiently, scratched Elvira under the chin and sighed. 'I just wish he'd be more honest,' she said in a very low voice, and I looked at her more closely, noticing the dark shadows under her eyes and the fine tension lines round her mouth.

'Is — is there anything I can do, to help in any way?' Maggie might make me feel frumpish and fat, but she was obviously unhappy, and right at that moment I knew how she felt.

'I shouldn't think so.' She glanced at me, then bit her lip quickly. 'Only, if you do happen to see him on his own, when the rest of the family aren't around, would you tell him I was here? It isn't really important except that, well, I've had some definite news, and I suppose he'd better hear about it.'

Somehow that reminded me of Barry's reference to skeletons in cupboards, but before I could say anything she'd scrambled to her feet as if she didn't want to be there any more and had already stayed too long.

I tried to get up, too, but the sun-lounger collapsed in on itself, and by the time I'd managed to convince Elvira this wasn't some new game I'd invented purely for her benefit, Maggie had gone as quietly and quickly as she'd appeared.

I stayed in the garden until Mrs Walker was back, hoping Sandie would come home, too, but when she rang to say she was having supper at Bev's, I excused myself before anyone could start asking a lot of awkward questions.

Mr Walker looked into my room once, to ask how school had been. And because I'd lied and told Mrs Walker I wasn't feeling very well because my period was due, she brought me some egg salad and bread-and-butter on a tray.

'Are you sure,' she fussed around, opening the window a little further and tweaking the curtains so they hung straight, 'you're okay, Juanita? Should we get a doctor or something?'

'I – I'll be fine,' I tried to assure her. 'This time of the month is always bad.'

That was another lie, and I wondered what was happening to me, but I wanted a good excuse to spend the evening on my own and that was the best one I could think of.

'Well, if you're positive?' She stopped picking things up and putting them down in different places, which had been making my head swim, and looked at me seriously.

'Listen, dear,' she perched on the edge of the dressing-table, swinging her legs in their blue jeans, and I suddenly noticed she painted her toenails pearl green. *My* mama would never do that. 'We *do* want you to enjoy your stay with us, and we do want you to be part of this crazy family.' She laughed nervously. 'I'm afraid I don't have much control over Sandie and Barry. I can't tell them what to do and what not to do, the way your parents probably can with you. They go their own way.

'I trust them,' she added simply, but I noticed she was wearing almost the same kind of worried face Maggie had had earlier. 'I trust them both to be as adult and sensible as they can be. It doesn't always work, particularly in Sandie's case where Robin Derwent's concerned. But I can't help feeling if I start interfering now and playing the heavy mother, it'll only make things very much worse. D'you understand?'

I didn't. In the slightest. But I nodded, because she obviously wanted me to.

'Then let Sandie sort out Robin in her own way. Though I gather,' she laughed, 'you've already made your feelings felt about the roses?'

I nodded and blushed, feeling extremely foolish. I should've realised Mrs Derwent would speak to Mrs Walker!

'Fair enough!' She got up and pulled her T-shirt down round her hips. 'Somebody probably should've done that to him years ago! I felt like stuffing the petals down his throat one by one!' she confided, and I gaped at her.

Barry had said his mother had thought Robin's gesture had been 'wonnerful', and yet now she was seriously telling *me* she'd have reacted exactly how *I'd* felt like reacting! Maybe Mrs Walker *did* realise her children weren't children any more!

'I'm sorry,' she added in a low voice as she walked towards the door, 'things haven't been easier since you arrived. Barry and Maggie, well . . .' She trailed off and nibbled her thumbnail thoughtfully. 'So little is actually *definite*, and it's difficult to know how to handle it all.

'I've never been a mum before.' She smiled as I watched her. 'I think my kids forget that. *They're* going through new experiences all the time – but so am I! Still, the books say it keeps you young! Now are you sure,' she turned the handle and the door opened a fraction, 'there isn't anything else I can get you?'

'Quite sure.' I grinned properly for the first time that day.

In a way Mrs Walker reminded me of my own mama. And suddenly England didn't seem quite so unfriendly any more.

Chapter 10

But Sandie continued not to talk to me for another ten days, which embarrassed everybody.

Whenever I came in, she made a point of going out with her nose in the air, or simply staring straight through me as if I didn't exist.

I didn't know whether to laugh or cry. She was my pen-friend, one of the main reasons for me being here at all, and when we'd been writing to each other we'd exchanged a lot of thoughts and dreams and hopes for our futures. But this was all so childish and unnecessary that I found myself spending an awful lot of time mumbling threats in Spanish to Robin Derwent under my breath.

Fortunately, although I was lonely a lot and had to try to hide it whenever I spoke to Mama or Papa, the school had arranged so many activities for us that I was hardly ever in the house anyway, and when I was I had to study.

'You're getting to be a complete stranger, y'know!' Barry joked when we passed on the stairs one morning. 'How was your day-trip to Hastings? See the place where old Harold copped it with the arrow through the eye?'

'Senlac Hill!' I felt proud of myself for remembering. 'We walked a lot. I sent Mama and Papa a postcard from Battle, and we went to Pett Levels at Winchelsea, but we didn't see the flamingos.' I shook my head sadly. I'd looked forward to seeing them after Miss Ellen had laughingly explained how the poor birds got it all confused and migrated *to* the nature reserve there instead of to a warmer country!

'Still, there was a house made from shells, and apple trees and plum trees in gardens in the middle of nowhere! Dieter said it was because the people had had their proper gardens flooded by the sea and were given other ones. But now they're overgrown. No one seems to use them any more.'

'Dieter?' Barry raised an interested eyebrow and grinned.

'Yes. In my class.' Stupidly I felt myself blush. I didn't feel anything for Dieter, except as a friend, but once or twice on that trip when we'd been walking round the cobbled streets in another small town called Rye, I'd stumbled, and he'd taken me by the arm to stop me falling. I'd thought then I'd have to be careful, because it seemed as if he liked me too much.

'So you've at least found someone to talk to? That's good.' Barry looked as if he wanted to say something else, probably about Sandie and the way she was behaving, but Mrs Walker suddenly shouted that there was a phone call for him and he galloped off downstairs.

'We're going to Stratford-upon-Avon, too!' I called after him, but if he heard me he didn't pay any attention and I trudged into my room feeling depressed and irritable.

Winchelsea and Rye had been pretty, the way I'd always imagined England would look.

Miss Ellen was enthusiastic about the Stratford trip, too. She'd shown us pictures of the Holy Trinity Church where Shakespeare was buried and explained how he'd become a Lay Rector – whatever that was – which allowed him to have his tomb in the chancel, *wherever* that was!

In her own way, she'd made him seem real to me, which he never had been before, and I'd wanted to try to explain that feeling to somebody English, like Barry.

I sat down hard on the end of the bed and thumped my fist against the mattress.

When I'd told Barry about Maggie's visit and given him the message she'd asked me to give him, he'd looked at me very coolly.

'Definite, is it?' he'd murmured. 'And what, precisely, d'you suppose she wants me to do now?'

'I – I don't know. Ring her, perhaps?'

'Perhaps.' The muscles in his face had tightened

for a second and he'd frowned angrily. 'How did she seem?'

'Nervous. Unhappy. Tired.' I'd shrugged. 'I'm not sure. I don't know her well enough.' I'd wanted to add that I didn't know what was going on, either, but I'd bitten the words back.

'Sometimes I wish I didn't know her at all! Remember what I told you about summers being fine and autumns changing everything?'

I'd nodded uncomfortably, but I don't think he'd even noticed because he'd turned away, scratching his head as if he were defeated.

'Well, this particular year,' he'd grunted bitterly, 'I can't wait to get through autumn and reach winter! I've got a feeling we'll all be a lot better off! Except, of course,' he'd managed to glance round and smile at me, '*you* won't be here.'

I'd carried that sentence around with me for days. I'd hugged it to me and gone over and over it in my mind, wondering if Barry was just being nice or if he'd really meant what he'd said.

'Juanita?'

I was lying on my bed and the door must've been open because I hadn't heard anyone come into the room. I gulped, trying to dredge up a smile from somewhere.

'Juanita, I just wanted to say – well, I'm really sorry. And I brought you these. Joe said you'd probably like them when we saw them in Northcote market this morning because they're so *English*. And Mum told me to bring them up to you.'

I felt the cool smoothness of something china being pushed into my hands – and when I looked up, Sandie was standing there with a foolish grin on her face, offering me a plate of strawberries and cream.

'I *am* sorry.' She sat down beside me while I stared at the strawberries. They were smothered in sugar and cream and impossible to eat without getting into a terrible mess because she'd forgotten to bring a spoon! 'I – I've been a idiot. Joe's made me understand that finally. But I, well, I guess I care about Robin too much and if he even looks at anybody else, I get jealous.'

'Yes.' I scooped up some cream with my finger and licked it. 'But he wasn't *looking* at me. Only showing off. Anyhow, I expect you've seen him many times recently?'

Why, oh why, I wondered, couldn't she sniff the real facts under her nose? Robin Derwent didn't care about her in the slightest. Robin Derwent very probably didn't care about anybody or anything except himself.

'Yes.' She fidgeted with some postcards I'd bought in Rye. 'But everybody else wants him, and he's picked me, and *I* want to hang on to him!'

I thought about the gentle, careful way Joe Berry had been with her when we'd brought her home that night, and sighed inside myself. I'd give anything in the world to have someone treat me the same way. Bunches of flowers and a lot of charm were one thing. Genuine caring was another.

'Anyway,' Sandie put the cards down, got to her feet and roamed round the room, 'I realise it was all because you're a stranger and everything, and I wanted to say I haven't any hard feelings any more!

'In fact,' she whirled round excitedly, 'I've even made an appointment with a beauty salon quite near your school tomorrow so I can have my ears pierced!

'I thought I could meet you, you could come with me, and then we'd go and have a pizza somewhere!'

I almost groaned out loud. Tomorrow I'd promised Dieter I'd see a film with him and have supper afterwards!

Chapter 11

In fact, when I woke the next morning my head felt as if Elvira's tail had been crashing into it all night, and I kept going hot and cold by turns.

It was probably a punishment for the lie I'd told about my period but Mrs Walker took one look at me as I pushed my breakfast cereal round the plate, came over and felt my forehead with the back of her hand.

'Young lady,' she announced, just as I dived for the door, hoping I could make the downstairs cloakroom before I was sick, 'you can forget about school and anything else today! You're going straight back to bed!'

'I – I'll be okay,' I stammered shakily, looking at my reflection in the tiny cloakroom's mirror. I was a greyish-green colour and reminded me of the way Sandie had looked after Robin's party.

'I'm sure you will!' Mrs Walker passed a warm face flannel through the door to me. 'But right at the moment you'll do as you're told!'

'It wasn't the strawberries, was it?' Sandie asked anxiously as I lay shivering under the duvet. 'I mean, I washed them and everything because Northcote's an open market and Mum always says all their fruit and veg get polluted by traffic fumes.'

'I don't think so.' The medicine Mrs Walker had made me swallow had at least stopped the sick feeling. 'You've heard of Spanish tummy?'

Sandie nodded seriously.

'Well,' I giggled weakly, and then wished I hadn't because it made my head hurt again, 'I think I've got an *English* tummy! I'll be okay. But Sandie,' I reached out and touched her hand tentatively, 'I'm sorry about not being able to come with you for your ears and everything.'

'That's okay,' she grinned. 'I've already rung Bev. *She's* coming. Then she's arranged it all to go on and meet your Dieter friend, if that's fine by you, and I'm meeting Robin!

'You see,' she was positively sparkling, 'it's all worked out in the end for everybody. Apart from poor old you, that is,' she added hastily, but I had the feeling she didn't really care that much about poor old me. Her mind was too full of other things.

I dozed for most of the rest of the morning feeling extremely sorry for myself and wondering what Dieter would make of Bev. Probably if she went on at him about awareness and the European countries helping each other in their time of crisis he'd forget his shyness and give her a lecture on how Germany was beating the economic recession, or whatever it was we were all supposed to be having!

'Perhaps they'll even,' I smiled sleepily to myself,

beginning to feel warmer at last, 'fall in love and get married! That'd be a *real* united peace policy!'

'How d'you think I look?'

I'd just closed my eyes when Sandie bounced into the room, pulled back the curtains Mrs Walker had closed earlier, and twirled at me.

She was wearing what can only be described as a long T-shirt with tassels, gathered at the waist by a broad leather belt, tan leg make-up that had blotched when she put it on, a pair of high-heeled sling-backs I recognised as her mum's, and far too much eye-shadow.

'It – it's certainly different!' I tried not to stare at her.

'Well, I thought, with my ears pierced – *and*,' she patted her head proudly, 'I'm having my hair done as well – when I meet Robin it'll be a whole new image!'

'Are you sure he'll recognise you?' I asked unkindly, then bit my bottom lip and smiled at her, hoping she hadn't realised what I'd said.

'I've *told* him,' she giggled, fiddling with her face at my dressing-table mirror, 'I'll be waiting outside Simpson's in Piccadilly and I'll have a scarlet rose behind my ear!

'I won't, of course.' She turned and blushed. 'But even if he doesn't recognise me, I'll know who *he* is, won't I? And that's the important thing!'

'Sandie . . .' I wanted to warn her to be careful. I wanted to tell her to forget Robin Derwent and take a closer look at Joe Berry instead, but when she threw me a questioning glance I lost my nerve and just shook my head. 'Nothing. Don't worry about it.

Have a good time. Have you decided on hoops or studs for your ears?'

'Studs.' She tightened the belt another notch and, because of the thin material of the T-shirt, she seemed to bulge out even more in the wrong places. 'Gold ones. Probably two sets to each ear, though don't mention that to Mum! And the stylist says she'll be able to straighten my hair as well as colour it! I'm going to look fantastic!'

She suddenly bent down and unexpectedly brushed her cheek against mine. 'See you later! Don't do anything I wouldn't!'

Then the bedroom door slammed loudly enough to take it off its hinges and I heard her heels clattering unevenly down the stairs.

I turned on my side and pulled the duvet cover over my head.

Sandie and I were the same age, in fact she was two months older than me and I'd always imagined she'd be much more grown-up and sophisticated, but the way she behaved made me feel very dull, and very, very ancient!

'Perhaps,' I murmured into the pillow, 'it's because I'm not in love! Perhaps you're only so stupid and fond of yourself when you are!'

'What're you muttering about? Have you decided to hibernate?'

Barry eased the cover back and peered at me curiously. I poked my tongue out at him.

'Fair enough!' He laughed and I felt the bed shake as he sat down. 'But a white tornado just left the house telling everyone it was going into town, and Mum thought you might like a glass of Lucozade and a plain biscuit to help give you strength –

presumably in case the white tornado comes back unexpectedly!' he added.

'White tornado? Oh, you mean Sandie?' I struggled up on to my arm.

'Who else?' he shrugged. '*You* didn't have anything to do with the way she looks, did you? I mean, this isn't a diplomatic illness, is it?'

'Diplomatic . . .?' I sipped some of the fizzy yellow-coloured drink and coughed because it tasted too sweet.

'When people don't want to go somewhere or do something,' he explained patiently, and I wondered for the umpteenth time why he bothered with me at all, 'they sometimes develop imaginary aches and pains that *stop* them going anywhere.

'If I'd encouraged Sandie to dress up as a sort of middle-class teenage tart, I think *I'd've* taken to my bed, too! But you didn't, did you?' He stared at me seriously, then his face relaxed as I shook my head.

'Sorry, little J.' He patted the duvet where my feet were and I wriggled my toes. 'But it did cross my mind you might want Robin Derwent to show himself in his true colours once and for all, which I strongly suspect he will do the second he sees Sandie, particularly if she develops bright green hair or something as well!'

I turned away.

I knew exactly what he meant. The same thoughts had crossed my mind, but as Sandie was only just being friendly to me again I hadn't wanted to upset her by telling her how cheap and awful she looked.

'Despite appearances,' he suddenly said thoughtfully, concentrating on a photograph of Mama and Papa I'd stuck up in the mirror, 'I'm quite fond of my little sister. I don't want anything dreadful to happen to her.'

I shivered, and Barry glanced towards me questioningly.

'Sorry. Nothing.' I tried to smile. 'Geese's pimples. But I think I ought to get up now. I can't stay here all day.'

I was feeling very embarrassed because I'd suddenly remembered I was only wearing a very short frilly nightdress which wasn't the sort of thing I should be talking to Barry in, and I hugged the quilt tighter round me, hoping he wouldn't notice how confused I must look.

'Juanita?' He shuffled his weight to the end of the bed and stared out through the window.

It was one of those soft grey days when the sun comes and goes, like the shutter of a camera clicking on and off the images you're looking at.

'Yes?'

'What d'you really think of us all? As people?'

'I – I think you're very nice.' I blushed and hid my face again.

'All of us? Or me, particularly? I seem to've talked to you more than anyone else.'

His voice seemed to come from a long way away and I closed my eyes. For some reason a picture of us standing in the neat strip of public gardens at the watchtower in Rye floated into my head.

It was so clear, so vivid, as if I'd moved Barry and myself into that setting from another time neither of us knew about yet, that I shivered again.

But *I* knew how we'd be. I knew how it would feel to have his hand cover mine. I knew how we'd smile, and how – when we kissed – we'd each catch fire from the other, holding on and breathing as if we were one person ...

And I also knew it could never happen.

'Juanita?' His hand, that brown hand with the gold hairs, pulled back the covers a little, and he frowned down at me. I hadn't even felt him move back up the bed.

'I – I think you, particularly, are nice and have perhaps been kindest to me,' I stammered. At least that was partially honest. 'I also think you are unhappy, and that this is to do with Maggie. And that Maggie is unhappy, which is to do with you.

'Your mother and father are like all mothers and fathers.' I took a deep breath and swallowed hard. 'They want what is best for everybody, but don't quite belong in our world because now they are too old. *Si?*'

Barry nodded and I realised his hand really *was* gripping mine, though how the two had got together I had no idea.

'And Sandie? Well,' I shrugged, feeling a cool draught round my shoulder as the quilt slipped slightly to one side, 'she is like me. She is busy growing up and making mistakes. It happens.'

With an enormous effort I wriggled my hand free from his and pulled the covers back closer. It was safer because I felt very small, very young and very vulnerable.

'Yes, I suppose it does.' His voice was so quiet I had to strain to hear him. 'Oh, Juanita!' He leaned further over and touched my partially hidden, frowning face. 'Why can't you be a couple of years older and not nearly as nice as you are?'

Then abruptly he got up and walked out of the room.

I lay where I was without moving for a long time. Then I turned on my back and squinted at the tiny particles of dust floating around on a watery shaft of sunlight.

I didn't understand, how *could* I understand, the things that were in everybody's minds.

These people were strangers and foreigners, and all I knew about any of them for certain was the sort of misty sadness they each carried around with them . . .

But if there had been sadness earlier, by late evening the atmosphere had changed to almost touchable anger.

There had been a telephone call for Barry earlier, so he'd done another of his disappearing tricks, and when Mr Walker had come home he and Mrs Walker had had a row in the kitchen about it which had made her rush upstairs in tears and shut herself in their room.

Because I was feeling better and was dressed I'd stayed very much out of the way by taking poor Elvira for a very long walk across the common.

'Come on, then!' I'd muttered eventually. 'Let's go back and see if Sandie's turned up yet.'

But Sandie hadn't, and by half-past ten I could tell from Mrs Walker's face she was feeling desperate.

'Perhaps they've gone to a late movie or the theatre or something?' I offered helpfully, but not too hopefully.

'And perhaps they haven't!' Mr Walker grunted, pouring himself another drink. 'I can't get hold of the Derwents. Their answering machine isn't even on. If it weren't for everything else that's happened recently,' he looked at his wife and frowned, 'I wouldn't even *be* worried. But Sandie could at least have rung us to tell us what she was up to!

'I'm sorry, Juanita. This is a hellish introduction to British life for you! Would you like a drink?'

I shook my head. I'd had some wine with supper. He'd clearly had one or two too many himself, and from Mrs Walker's tight-lipped expression she didn't want to encourage him to have any more.

The front door slammed and we all froze. The only things in the room that seemed to move were Elvira's ears as they twitched forward, listening.

Lopsided footsteps I recognised as Sandie's crossed the hall slowly, and I stood up.

'Please?' I looked at the two parents, suddenly realising how many times in different ways my own parents must have worried like this about me. 'Let me go and see her. If something is wrong, then she may talk to me. If all is well and she is just ashamed for being late, then,' I shrugged, 'I'll bring her in here.'

Mrs Walker nodded slowly, twisting her hands together so hard her rings must've dug into her.

Mr Walker straightened his back and cleared his throat, as if he were trying to decide whether he was angry or relieved. And I went towards the door with Elvira padding behind me.

Sandie was sitting on the third bottom step of the stairs.

Her dress was crumpled. Her bubbly hair was sleeked down into a stern boyish crop that didn't suit her in the slightest, and the ends were tinted a deep purple.

She'd broken one of the heels off her mother's sling-backs, and she was holding it carefully, as if it

were the most precious treasure on earth, while she
cried her eyes out.

Chapter 12

A cold, sickly panic shot through me and I stood very
still, wondering what to do or say. Elvira had already
trotted across to her and was whimpering as she
licked at the sticky mascara-coloured tears.

'Hi.' She looked up and tried to smile. 'How're
you feeling?'

'Much better. *You* look terrible.'

'Probably.' She put the shoe down and began
fiddling with the other one. 'But at least I've got holes
in my ears now. Look!'

I went over and she moved so I could sit on the
step beside her.

'Your new ear-rings will be nice when you wear
them. You must send me a photograph of you then,
so I can see for myself.'

'Yes. The woman said I had to keep the studs in
for a least four weeks, and you'll be gone by then,
won't you?'

'Long before.' It was a peculiar conversation to be
having in the dimly-lit hall but I didn't know what
else to do. Whatever had happened to her wasn't
something I felt I could force out of her. 'Would you
like me to make you some coffee?'

'Are Mum and Dad in?' She sniffed and wiped her

hand across her face which smeared the mascara down her cheeks.

'I'm afraid so. There has been some kind of row, and they've been worried about you.'

'Oh.' She closed her eyes tightly and I knew she was holding back more tears. 'Is there going to be another row now I'm back?'

'I don't know.' I shook my head, got to my feet and pulled her gently to hers. 'Let's go into the kitchen. Or would you like to wash and change first?'

'Mmm.' She nodded listlessly, her whole body hanging in on itself as if she were a dead rag-doll.

'Then go!' I was surprised at the authority in my own voice. 'I think your hair will be enough of a shock for them without seeing the rest of you like this!'

I watched as she dragged herself up towards her own room, then I took Elvira by the collar and walked her through to the kitchen.

'Well?' Mr Walker followed me in and was tapping his foot impatiently as I plugged in the electric coffee machine. 'What's wrong? Is she all right?'

'I think so.' I didn't want to look at him and I was glad I was busy doing something. 'She is changing.'

All I wanted him to do was go away and give me some time alone with Sandie. I might not be able to help her, but from what I'd seen of her she'd be calmer if she talked to me first instead of her parents.

'Five minutes!' Mr Walker threw me a warning look as if he'd read my mind. 'No more. Then *we* want some sort of explanation.'

'Yes of course.' I spooned sugar into a mug. 'But please,' I faced him, hoping he'd understand that I knew I was a guest in his home but that I truthfully wanted to help, 'when you do, could you not talk about her hair? It is,' I hesitated, 'a rather peculiar colour in places, and you won't like it!'

'If that's all that's wrong I won't even mind!' He tried to laugh, then went unsteadily back towards the lounge.

I heard the door click firmly shut, and Sandie must have too because seconds later she shuffled in, barefoot, and sat down wearily at the table.

'What happened?' I put the mug of strong coffee in front of her and watched as she took the first sip.

'Everything was fine.' She struggled to swallow. 'Bev came with me while I had my hair done. What d'you think of it, by the way?' She patted it self-consciously.

'It's hideous!' I shrugged truthfully. 'But you can always have it dyed back. But tell me, what else happened?'

'Well,' she sloshed the coffee round in the mug, staring down at it, 'she stayed while they fired the studs into my ears. That didn't hurt as much as I'd thought it would, and I felt tremendous when we left. Sort of tall and glamorous and mysterious.'

She looked very small and crumpled and tear-stained.

'Then you met Robin?' I prompted, and she nodded.

'He told me I wasn't the same old Sandie at all, which was the whole idea, and we went along to meet some friends of his in a club in Soho.'

Inside myself, I groaned. I'd only walked round Soho in daylight, but I could imagine what kind of club she might've found herself in.

'That was a laugh, actually. I mean,' she glanced

at me uneasily, 'it wasn't full of strippers or anything, just heavy music and booze and the odd funny cigarette. Robin wanted me to have one but I didn't. I'm not *that* stupid!

'Then,' she took a deep breath, 'we went on to a flat one of the older guys shares in Bayswater, and that's where it all went wrong.'

'Wrong?' My stomach was turning over again, but it had absolutely nothing to do with whatever had upset me that morning.

'Yes. Robin wanted — well, he wanted me to go off with him alone. He said to stop kidding around because that was obviously what *I* wanted, too. We had a fight.' She suddenly put her head in her hands and howled, 'he was *awful*, Juanita! He grabbed me and kissed me very hard, he didn't even *try* to be gentle!'

'What else did he do?' Barry's voice cut through the silence in the room like a razor slashing butter. I'd had my back to the kitchen door and neither of us had heard him come in.

'Well?' He strode across to his sister and shook her roughly. 'Tell me, because once I've heard the rest of this sordid little story, I've every intention of going round to knock his stupid head off!'

'Please, Barry!' Without realising what I was doing I grabbed him and tried to pull him away from Sandie. 'This won't do any good.'

'Nothing happened.' Sandie sounded dull and empty. 'But even if it had, Barry, *you* can't really talk, can you?'

For a second I thought he was going to hit her and I clutched at him even more tightly. But then his entire body sagged and he sank down in the other chair and put his free arm round her.

'Fair enough, love,' he whispered. 'But that's different, and you know it. What's happened to you is just, well . . . outlandish.'

'I – I thought he loved me!' Sandie looked up, tears falling everywhere.

'The rest of us, even Juanita, knew he was using you. The Derwents may be friends of Mum and Dad's, but Robin's just a low-grade little sod who fancies his chances with anything in a skirt!'

'I – I know – now. He and his friends just laughed because I got angry – it made me feel dirty. I – I ran away. I couldn't get a taxi to bring me all the way here, so I got one to Victoria and caught the tube home. That's it.' She slumped against her brother. 'Robin's probably still there making jokes about me!'

'For his sake, I hope he *stays* there!' Barry growled, then glanced at me. 'Nip through and ask Dad to pour a brandy for her, J. Tell them I'm here and she's okay and I'll be in in a minute.'

'Right,' I nodded worriedly. 'But won't they want to know what's happened?'

'Tell them,' Barry sounded very grown-up and firm, 'I'll explain everything once I've got her into bed. And you, Sandie,' he took his arm away and made her look at him, 'stop acting like a tragedy-queen.

'Thank God,' he went on, 'it stopped where it did stop. Anything else would probably've finished Mum completely! As kids, we're being none too bright at the moment. But I've learned a couple of lessons the hard way, and maybe you've learned one, too?'

'Y-yes.' She struggled to smile at him, then turned to me. 'And Juanita, I *am* sorry, for ruining your

78

holiday and everything!' Before either of us could stop her she got to her feet and dashed upstairs.

I stood still, wondering if I should do what Barry had asked me to do.

My head hurt and part of me wished I could run away, too – home to Spain, where I could forget all about English summers.

Perhaps I was learning things as well, but whatever they were, I knew I wouldn't be able to make sense of them for a month or so.

Barry simply sat, staring down at the splodges Sandie's tears had left on the polished table, and I finally tiptoed past him, told Mr and Mrs Walker what he'd said to tell them, and once I'd put the brandy in front of him for Sandie, excused myself in a low voice and said I was going to bed.

'J?' His hand suddenly shot out and caught mine. 'I don't think Sandie should be left to wander around on her own for a couple of days. Is there any way you can cut some of the school outings and spend a bit of time with her?'

'I suppose so.' I wanted to tell him that I was only going on all the outings because I didn't want the Walkers to feel they had to entertain me all the time.

'I'll organise a trip or something for the weekend – a picnic at Henley, maybe. You can ask your Dieter friend if he'd like to come, and I'll get Joe Berry to show up for Sandie.'

'And you?' That seemed very important. 'Who will you bring?'

'Myself and my universally-known charm! Don't worry about me.' He bent down, buried his head in Elvira's neck and ruffled her fur.

I don't know what happened for the rest of that

evening.

I could hear raised voices and doors slamming. The telephone rang a couple of times, and because Sandie's room was next to mine I could hear her sobbing and Mrs Walker talking to her softly.

But when I went down next morning, the house was deserted.

Mr Walker had left a note pinned to the shopping-list board saying that Sandie and her mother had gone out for the day, but that Barry would be in and around and if I wanted anything just to ask him for it.

I caught the tube to Victoria, and instead of going on from there the way I normally did, I got hopelessly lost and eventually wound up wandering through Green Park in the bright sunshine and wondering if anyone would notice if I didn't show up at the school at all.

But Dieter was waiting for me when I walked into the reception area, and he hurried towards me with a broad grin on his face.

'I am so pleased,' he grasped both my hands warmly, 'to find you well again. The friend of your friend, Beverley, said you had caught something.'

'Just a chill,' I grinned back. He was flushed and his eyes had that extra-bright sparkle you usually only see in people something wonderful has just happened to.

'I also wish to thank you,' he pulled me towards a corner bench, 'for my meeting Beverley. She is *most* interesting. Most interesting indeed, yes!' His head was bouncing up and down in excitement. 'I am to see her this lunchtime and she will show me the grave of Karl Marx in Highgate Cemetery. This place also,' he was almost dancing, 'has the tomb of a lion-tamer, which is shaped like a lion, and Charles Dickens's wife is buried there!

'On Saturday,' he was hardly stopping to draw breath and was making me feel dizzy, 'we go to another famous burial ground in south London. Is not all this wonderful?'

'Amazing!' I smiled. I'd never seen anybody get so excited by the prospect of going round a lot of old tombs before, but I strongly suspected it had more to do with Bev herself than with the places!

'So' — and to my complete surprise he suddenly kissed me on the cheek — 'this English holiday is being terrific, isn't it?'

I was glad for Dieter, really glad, but I couldn't help wishing, as I watched him race through the school doors to meet Bev, that something terrific would happen to me soon, too!

Because there didn't seem much point in hurrying back after classes, I went to Covent Garden instead and walked round the shops buying little gifts for Dolores and Katerine.

I knew, at home, I'd have to pretend to them that I'd had a wonderful time and met thousands of different people, all of whom had fallen desperately in love with me. Well, I could hardly tell them the truth, could I? That *no one* had fallen in love with me, but that *I* had, and that it hurt because it was hopeless.

When I finally came out of somewhere calling itself The Body Shop, the afternoon had clouded over and a thin, persistent rain was soaking everywhere.

I was only wearing jeans and a sleeveless top, and I shivered, brushing my hair out of my face and wondering which was the quickest way to the Walkers' from where I was.

I pulled my *A-Z of London* out of my bag and was standing frowning at the map, trying to see which street I was in, when two hands suddenly went round my waist and someone said, 'Now what is a gorgeous girl like you doing getting soaked in a place like this?'

My first impulse was to scream and look for a policeman, but the hands slid away from my waist and one of them patted me on the bottom.

'I'm with some mates. We've got a car parked in Long Acre. We could take you on a sightseeing tour if you like. How about it?'

I wriggled free. Not only was I soaking wet, but every part of me seemed to crawl from Robin Derwent's over-familiar touch, and without thinking twice I lifted my right arm and slapped him firmly across his too-good-looking, leering face.

'Now what,' he gasped, staggering back while a couple of passers-by grinned at us in amusement, 'was *that* for?'

'Sandie!' I spat, then turned on my heel and started to run down towards the Strand.

Chapter 13

Fortunately a taxi drew up by the traffic lights at the Savoy Hotel and I jumped in and asked it to take me to Victoria Station, then sat back in the cold leather seat and closed my eyes tightly.

I was still feeling confused and shaky when I finally unlocked the door of the Walkers' home, praying neither Sandie nor her mother would be back yet from wherever they'd gone.

I didn't want to have to tell them about that meeting with Robin, or about what I'd done to him, but I knew perfectly well if there was anybody there my face would give itself away.

The rain clouds and general darkness of the afternoon seemed to press down at my head, and I fumbled round for the light-switch in the kitchen, muttering to myself in Spanish and tripping over Elvira who was woofing and wagging her tail enthusiastically.

'I'll take you out in a moment!' I told her, towelling my hair dry. 'But I've got to change first, otherwise I'll catch pneumonia!'

She was desperate to play and she grabbed at the end of the towel as I rubbed my neck, so we both overbalanced and wound up sitting on the floor facing each other foolishly.

'Oh, Elvira!' I reached across and patted her. 'I wish my life were as simple as yours! It must be nice to be a dog and have everybody make your decisions for you.'

'Yes, it must, mustn't it?' Maggie suddenly said quietly from the shadows, and I scrambled to my knees, feeling an utter idiot. Just when you thought you were alone, the Walkers and their friends seemed to pounce out at you.

'I – I'm sorry. I didn't realise anyone was here!' I let Elvira have the towel and she carried it off into a corner, growling at it and shaking it from side to side as if it were some huge prize.

'That's okay. But you're right. You had better change. You're soaked.' She sounded very tired and not at all self-possessed. 'Go and do it now. I'll make a cup of tea, if you like?'

She got up slowly, rubbing her back as if it hurt. 'And don't look so alarmed. You've every right to be here and I haven't, but I'm not burgling the place. I just dropped in on the off-chance of meeting Barry.'

'I — I gave him your last message.' That seemed years ago and I shifted uncomfortably from foot to foot.

'Yes, I know.' She smiled, but it stopped at her lips. 'I gather there's been a bit of fuss and bother with Sandie and Robin Derwent?'

'You could say that!' I flushed scarlet, remembering how completely and utterly *happy* I'd been to slap Robin's face. 'So then, you've seen Barry already?'

She shook her head and fiddled with the kettle. 'I met Joe on my way over. I really should give Barry his key back, I suppose.'

I wanted to confide in her that *I'd* seen Robin, and that absolutely nothing had changed about him. I wanted to blurt out all the things Barry had said to Sandie last night about neither of them being too bright at the moment — but something in her face stopped me.

'Sandie's an idiot!' Maggie muttered, pulling a box of tea-bags out of the cupboard. It was as if she lived there. 'If she could look further than Robin's manly chest,' the words were emphasised sarcastically, 'she'd see Joe Berry worships the ground she walks on!

'And I'm a fool, too. If anything, a bigger one than

Sandie! You'd think somebody who works for the social services would actually know what to do about *themselves*, wouldn't you?'

'Is that what you do?' I asked curiously.

'Sure!' She plonked the tea-bags into two mugs. 'I'm even taking my Certificate of Social Work, or I was supposed to be,' she added mysteriously.

'I'm sorry.' I was, too. Somehow I'd imagined Maggie was just another beautiful empty-headed secretary who wanted to be a model or a pop-star. I hadn't thought, for one minute, she'd be doing anything *serious*. 'Where d'you work?'

'A funny little building that's more like a garage than a social centre. I'm supposed to have a "way with children", you see!' she laughed bitterly, poured boiling water into the mugs and turned to look at me. 'Why all the interest anyway?'

'I'm sorry,' I stammered again. 'It's just that, well I know so little about anyone, except *who* they are and how they seem to me.'

'There's not a lot else to know. Sandie's a pretty ordinary sixteen-year-old who spends her time falling in love and dreaming about white weddings.'

'And Barry?' I sat down, forgetting I was still wet and cold.

'Barry?' She shrugged. 'Ah, Barry! He's extremely clever, extremely imaginative, and extremely good at dealing with people. He dreams of working for the BBC on their overseas broadcasts, because he's good at languages and wants to travel. But he's got this chance to study for a year in France. I think he should take it. Wouldn't you?'

'It depends.' I felt uncomfortable, and it wasn't just because I was shivering. 'Perhaps there's something else? Something he thinks is much more important?'

'Oh,' Maggie sat down opposite me and cradled her mug in her hands, 'there is something he thinks is much more important. He thinks,' she gulped her tea and stared out at the rain-washed garden bleakly, 'it's more important to marry me because he has to!'

'Sorry?' I didn't understand.

'*Has* to.' She put the mug down and some of the tea spilled, reminding me of Sandie's tears last night. 'You mean none of the family's given out the joyous news yet? I'm pregnant! I'm going to have a baby. Barry's baby! And Sir Galahad,' she got up quickly and tried to rescue my towel from Elvira, 'thinks he ought to do the decent thing!

'So does his mother. So does his father. So, come to that, does *my* mother – but then, she would, wouldn't she?' It wasn't really a question to be answered, just a statement of fact.

'What would *you* do, Juanita?' She pulled the towel away from the dog and put it down on top of a work-surface, then looked at me directly. 'If it were you?'

'I – I wouldn't have a choice.' I drank some of my own tea and tried to make the whirling, confusing statements I'd been hearing make sense. 'It would be expected I become married. I – I've never thought.'

'Nobody ever does!' Maggie said bitterly. 'You always think it can't possibly happen to you because you've taken all the proper precautions, and anyway you love the person so what does it matter?

'But when it's all real, when it's something that's inside you and growing, you *have* to think, and everything has to matter!'

'But if you *do* love each other?'

'Oh, I love him all right. I think he even loves me. But we're only twenty! I can't let him sacrifice the rest of his life because we made a mistake!'

'The mistake *belongs* to both of you.' I didn't know what else to say, it was so obvious. 'You're going to have the baby?'

'Oh yes.' She hugged herself and a little smile flitted across her face. 'I'm not really into the alternative.'

'Then you should marry each other.' It seemed remarkably simple. 'Why should there be sacrifices? You can continue to study, and when the baby is born, perhaps you can *all* go to France, until Barry finds the kind of work he wants most,' I added hopefully.

'And how do the three of us live?' Her smile had disappeared. 'How d'you think it'll all be in a few years' time if he loses his opportunities now? We'll be at each other's throats like – like Elvira and Tiddlykins! I saw that happen with my own mum and dad, thanks. Then one day he just walked out because he couldn't take it any more. I don't want to see it happen again!'

'But,' I felt like telling her she was being sillier and younger even than me or Sandie, 'it *needn't* happen. Not if you both talk. Not if you both care enough.'

'And we'll only know if we care enough when we're married, is that what you mean?'

We both spun round and I gulped, wishing the floor would conveniently open up and swallow me.

Barry was standing in the kitchen doorway, his anorak dripping rain into small puddles on the floor and his eyes fixed firmly on Maggie's miserable face. Neither of them said another word. He just held open his arms and she walked slowly into them, all the tears she'd been trying to hold back suddenly rushing over.

'I *do* love you,' she whispered into his chest, burrowing against him the way an animal does from the winter winds. 'And I don't want to destroy you.'

'You couldn't.' His voice was very warm and soft and he helped her carefully into a chair then squatted down beside her, still holding her. Both of them had completely forgotten I was there. 'And *I* don't want to destroy any of us. You're much too important and I love you much too much, even though nobody else thinks we're old enough to know our own minds.'

I didn't wait to hear any more. Somehow, at last, they'd begun their talking process, and as I tiptoed past, hushing Elvira to keep her quiet, I felt myself smile.

Their baby, I thought, would be greatly loved. And their marriage, even if it *was* too soon, too much at the wrong time, might last them for the rest of their lives.

It was only when I was sitting in the pale room upstairs thinking and wondering and trying to make sense of everything I'd been learning that I realised Barry had been wearing a suit, shirt and tie under the wet anorak. With anyone else, it wouldn't've been surprising. With him, for a reason I couldn't pinpoint, it was.

Chapter 14

Maggie stuck her head round my door about an hour later and smiled at me, a full, relaxed smile that drove away all the tired lines.

'Just wanted to say thanks,' she murmured. 'And apologise for all the times I've been nasty.'

'You weren't,' I smiled back, closing my book. 'And there's nothing to thank me for!' I spread my hands and shrugged. 'I didn't do anything.'

'You did, you know.' She hesitated in the doorway. 'You said things aloud that Barry and I had been thinking but we were both so uptight we didn't know how to say them to each other, so we just argued and shouted instead. Anyway,' she scraped her foot shyly back and forward across the carpet, 'we're going to get it all arranged now, the wedding and everything. I don't suppose you can stay on for it? It can't really happen for another month.'

'No.' I shook my head. 'By then I must be home, because school will be starting and I have to prove how good my English is to everyone!' I pulled a face. 'But I will send a card and think about you on the day. Perhaps you might even come to Spain next year?' It was my turn to feel shy again. 'Mama *loves* babies! Yours would be very safe with her while you and Barry had a – a,' I blushed stupidly, 'honeymoon.'

'Oh, Juanita!' She suddenly crossed the room in three quick strides, threw her arms round me and gave me an enormous hug. 'You really *are* a super girl! Did you know that?'

'I am me.' I was very embarrassed and I squirmed

away, not knowing what to do or say next.

'That's what I mean!' She smiled again, then quickly patted me on the shoulder. 'I've got to dash now and I probably won't see you again before Saturday, but we'll have a great day out, I promise.'

'Saturday?' I didn't understand.

'Yes.' She paused, looking very beautiful and radiant with her hand on the door. 'Barry's going to borrow the estate car and we're all going to have that picnic. As you've missed your Stratford trip, we thought we'd start out early and drive there, just so you can say you've been there when you get home. It should be fun! We'll have lunch by the river and feed bread to the swans. How does that grab you?'

It grabbed me quite nicely, apart from the sudden pang of loneliness that shot through me. Maggie would have Barry. Sandie would no doubt have Joe. But I would be the odd one out. The stranger who didn't quite belong.

'See you then, then!' She blew me a kiss, and I heard her feet clattering down the stairs.

I sat where I was for what felt like quite a long time, staring through the window over the gardens.

I watched Elvira plod round the lawn, sniffing the clean smells and then suddenly woofing and rolling over and over in the damp grass, her tail wagging crazily and her face looking very surprised every time she discovered she was a different way round to the way she'd been before.

I was just beginning to drift off into a daydream where I was back home and running along the surf, hand in hand with a boy whose face I couldn't see, when there was another tap at the door, followed by Barry saying, 'Juanita? Can I ask you another favour?'

'Favour?' I blinked and turned. He was still wearing his suit, but he'd taken off the tie and loosened his collar.

'Mmm.' He slumped on the bed looking completely exhausted. 'Y'see, I've got to go shopping, and I *hate* shopping. I wondered,' now he was the one who was blushing, 'whether you could maybe spare the time to come with me tomorrow? I don't want to tell the rest of the family about Maggie and me yet, and I do,' he was like a little boy caught with cream trifle he's been told not to eat all over his face, 'want to buy her a ring! But I'm going to need help.'

'Then why on earth,' I giggled, 'don't you take *Maggie*? Isn't that more usual?'

'Probably. When the circumstances aren't the way they are for us. But I want it to be a surprise. I've got her size and everything,' he blushed even harder, 'and I thought I could maybe use your fingers – *and* your advice – when it finally got down to the nitty-gritty!'

'Oh Barry!' I wasn't giggling any more. I was laughing aloud. All the lonely thoughts had been driven away into the sunlight. 'Of course I'll come with you. I'd be delighted to, if that's the way you say it. But,' I sat down beside him, 'I won't move a step unless you tell me one thing!'

'What's that?' Alarm shot across his face.

'Why,' I fingered the material of his jacket, 'are you wearing a suit? You look like a trainee bank manager, very proper and very grown-up!'

'Yes, well,' he growled and I laughed again, 'I had an interview this morning. And that's something *else*,' he waggled his finger warningly under my nose, 'I don't want to tell anybody yet, not even Maggie. I was hoping I could get in and back to normal before I was spotted.'

'Oh.' I didn't know whether to ask any more questions or not, but he was tapping his fingers against his knees as if he wanted to bruise himself, so I took a deep breath. 'Was – was it successful?'

I got up quickly. Somehow I knew it would be better if I had my back to him when he answered, then his face could allow itself to do whatever it wanted to do.

'Hopeful. The great British Broadcasting Corporation think they could maybe train me to eventually work for their overseas programmes.

'I sent in the application form yonks ago, before all this Maggie business even happened. Y'see,' I heard him get up and move towards me, 'I've been in love with Maggie for the last two years. I've wanted us to get engaged at least, but there wasn't a lot of point in doing that while we were both still studying. Also Mum and Dad were so pleased and proud of me being in college I kind of felt I owed it to them to carry on. But well, Maggie is Maggie, and I didn't want to lose her.

'The job for the Beeb was advertised earlier this year. I applied because I thought, well, it could lead towards what I really want to do. I don't just want to wind up as a language teacher in some grotty school, Juanita. Does that make sense?'

It only just did because I wasn't too sure what he was talking about, but I nodded, knowing he needed to go on.

'I – I also thought,' he scratched his chin and stared down at the garden, 'if I at least *had* a job, I could ask Maggie to marry me.

'I knew the actual *wedding* couldn't happen for a couple of years, not until I'd a bit more cash behind me so we could start off decently in our own place, but I wanted her around *permanently*,' he stressed the word with an awful lot of love in his voice, 'and although I knew Mum and Dad would be furious if I jacked in college, I reckoned they'd come round in time if they could see I was really making something for myself.

'I didn't hear anything from the BBC so I just assumed they'd filed my application in their waste-paper basket, and I agreed to this year's language exchange instead.

'Then Maggie discovered she was pregnant and we both panicked. I felt trapped. But yesterday,' he smiled at me softly, 'the Beeb rang while everybody was busy doing something else and asked me along for an interview today. Hence,' he gestured to himself, 'the suit. Answer all the questions?'

'Oh yes,' I whispered, a bubble of excitement for him building up inside me. 'But when will you know definitely?'

'The end of the week, but they've more or less said there'll be something for me on a trial basis if I want it. The money won't be wonderful, but it'll be better than the dole, and it'll mean the three of us,' he smiled again and I closed my eyes, seeing him with a baby under one arm and a teddy-bear under the other, '*can* have a solid beginning.

'But J.,' he turned and put his fingers against my lips, 'not a word to anyone else yet. Okay?'

'Okay,' I murmured, another surge of different, conflicting thoughts crashing through my head. 'We'll have a secret.' I moved away quickly in case he should guess some of what was going through my mind. 'And tomorrow we'll go shopping. Now, where,' I tried to make my voice sound lighter and less quivery, 'is Sandie? Has she come home yet?'

'Yup!' he grinned, easing his suit-jacket off. 'She's downstairs with almost normal hair again and a very mouse-like expression on her face. She said to tell you that she's going round to see Joe and won't be very long.

'Maybe she's come to her senses, too,' he added thoughtfully.

I was glad Barry wasn't in for supper that night because if he had been I don't think I'd've been able to keep the secret between us. As it was, I kept grinning to myself like an idiot and having to suddenly hide my face in a serviette.

Sandie was very quiet, and Mr and Mrs Walker were exchanging secret glances and messages that really made me feel we'd all be better out of the way so *they* could talk to each other, too.

We all watched television for a bit, then I went upstairs and started to wrap some of the gifts I'd bought for the people at home.

In another ten days I'd be back in my own room with the sound of the sea outside the windows and Mama singing to herself in the kitchen.

I'd listen to my music tapes with the headphones on so Papa wouldn't get angry, and I'd finally have to tell Dolores and Katerine all about the English summer and the places I'd been and the people I'd met.

But, I wondered as I put some of the packages into my case, how would I really *feel*? I wasn't at all the same person who'd got off that Iberia plane. Although nothing had actually happened to *me* – everything had happened around me.

Ever since I'd started growing up I'd imagined that falling in love and getting married and finally having children would be what I would do.

Now, I wasn't so sure.

I wanted to fall in love, yes! Of course I did! Not just once – but twice, three times, a hundred times! I wanted romance and happiness and a lot of silly laughter. But I was still far, far too young to face the problems Maggie and Barry were having to face. And there was still far too much – even although I didn't know what most of it was yet – I needed to do with the rest of my life.

Chapter 15

The next few days went past in such a complete whirl that I was exhausted!

Sandie, who'd got some of her bounciness back with her curly hair, arranged for Joe and herself and me to go on a riverboat from the Houses of Parliament to Windsor, and for the first time since I'd arrived in London I felt like a proper tourist, taking photographs of everything the guides said was important, or very historical, or just very English.

'Incidentally,' Sandie sidled up to me and grinned as I was trying to focus my camera on what I'd been told was Putney Bridge, 'what's all this about you going shopping with Barry? He was really cheesed when I told him I'd arranged this for today.'

'Oh!' My hand flew to my mouth. 'It's just that,' I floundered around looking for some kind of excuse, then took a deep breath and lied through my teeth, 'he said he'd help me find something for Papa, to take home with me.'

'Humph!' Sandie flounced her hair at a passing American boy in a terrible shirt. 'Well, as long as that's *all* you're doing! You're *my* friend, remember! Not his! Even though he *has* set up everything for Saturday, hasn't he, Joe?' She grabbed Joe's arm and he grinned at her.

'Certainly! And it's time Juanita had a decent day out. All those school lectures and studying she's been doing must be making her brain go numb! Now just shut up, Sandie, and behave! Okay?' He kissed her on the cheek then and she threw her arms round his neck, kissing his face back until their lips met and held in a much longer, proper kiss.

I left them to it and walked over to the other side of the boat. Sandie had been an idiot. She probably *would* be an idiot again in the future and I'd read all about it in her letters. But I had the feeling, as long as Joe was around to love her and keep an eye on her, she'd also be all right.

That night, when we got back to the Walkers', Barry was waiting for me in the hallway and he hissed furiously, '*Tomorrow*? Okay? Maggie's coming with us on Saturday and I want her to have it by then. We'll be back here afterwards, as well, so I'd *better* have it by then!'

'Okay! Okay!' I grinned, and in the morning he

and I slipped out after Mr and Mrs Walker had gone to work and before Sandie was up.

'Where are we going?' I asked as he fastened me into the seatbelt in his car. 'The West End?'

'Come off it, J.!' He fastened his own belt, switched on the engine and pulled carefully into the street. 'I can't afford Cartiers, you know! But there's a place in Streatham that does antique as well as modern stuff. I thought we could try there.'

He must have worked very hard at all his part-time jobs after college and during the vacations, because the engagement ring he eventually bought for Maggie had eight small diamonds set round a central diamond, and although it didn't cost anything like Princess Diana's, he still handed over nearly two hundred pounds in cash!

'Shouldn't you,' I said shyly when we left the shop, 'have kept some of that money? For when you are married and everything?'

'No.' He took my arm and shook his head positively. 'Now come on, there's something else I want to show you.'

We got back into the car and drove round another huge piece of green-treed common, then along a lot of small side streets full of tall, narrow, side-by-side buildings, until he eventually drew to a stop outside a tiny house with an even tinier piece of garden.

A black cat was sitting on the low wall washing itself, and it miaowed as Barry and I walked through the rusty wrought-iron gate.

I glanced at him. He grinned and produced a key from his pocket. 'Not exactly a palace,' he murmured, unlocking the door. 'But home. See what you think.'

I stood in the cramped, dim hall and stared round me. It was like being inside a dolls' house. Everything was small, even the bath in the bathroom, but the walls had been papered and painted, there were carpets on the floor, and when he opened the door from the kitchen onto the paved yard, even the stone tubs and window boxes were brilliant with flowers.

'Well?' he asked anxiously, while I stared and stared. 'Will she like it? There's a separate room for the baby. It's not very big, but then neither are babies, are they?'

'You mean,' I gulped, 'it's *yours*?'

'Ours!' he corrected me. 'We'll probably have to sit on orange-boxes and sleep on the floor! And I haven't bought it, before you start thinking I'm some kind of millionaire! It's only rented.' He blushed and I thought for the millionth time what a nice person he was. 'This is where I've been disappearing to such a lot. It was in a terrible state so some of my mates gave me a hand to do it up.'

'And if Maggie and you hadn't got together in the end?'

He shrugged. 'There're always people looking for somewhere to live in London. I'd've found one of them and then taken off for the great unknown. I was lucky to get it in the first place, friend of a friend and all that,' he added hastily. 'But d'you think it'll do? To start, I mean?'

'Oh Barry!' I couldn't help it. I threw my arms round him and hugged him. 'When do you bring her to show her? You must,' I was excited, 'put flowers in every room! *I* will do that! And – and,' I searched round in my mind for the most romantic idea I could think of, 'buy a large teddy-bear with a bow round its neck and have a bottle of champagne on ice! Then,' my imagination was working overtime, 'you carry her over the threshold and tell her it is hers!'

I hugged him again, skipping from foot to foot. To my surprise, he hugged me back, then pushed me away a little, took me by the hand and led me back through the little house towards the car.

'Make me one promise, Juanita,' he said sternly as I settled into my seat, and I frowned at him. 'Promise me that if, *ever*, somebody in Spain — or anywhere else in the world that you happen to be — ever hurts you very badly, you'll let Maggie and me know. Because I, for one,' he gunned the car into life, 'will find him and strangle him! You're a sweetheart of a person. Don't ever change!'

Chapter 16

When we got back Mrs Walker was making lunch, but she raised an eyebrow at us both and then said, 'Juanita, your mother rang. Something about a wedding or an engagement. I didn't quite understand it. Can you call her back? I think she'd like you to go home earlier than you intended.'

Mama was bubbling over with news, and even the crackles on the telephone line couldn't take away how pleased she sounded.

'Katerine!' she giggled at me, while I tried to think Spanish, not English. 'She is finally engaged to Paco!

99

There is a big party. Papa has arranged everything. This time next week you will be home! The airline has guaranteed you a ticket, and I convinced Papa you would want to be with your friend for her party and had been working so hard you should have some holidays here. Are you glad? I look forward to seeing you so much!'

I didn't know what to say.

Part of me *was* glad to be going home, but not for the reasons Mama would imagine. It would be wonderful to see her and Papa, of course. But Katerine? Engaged? Like me, she was too young to know her own heart. How *could* she get engaged? Paco had always been her father's choice, and she liked him. But I suddenly doubted if she loved him – the way I'd seen love properly work between Maggie and Barry.

'Everything okay?' Barry touched me on the shoulder and frowned as I put down the telephone.

'Next week.' I shrugged. 'I go. I have no choice. Papa has already arranged it.'

And that night, for the first time in my life, I lay in the dark and told Papa through my thoughts that, sooner or later, he had to let me properly grow up; that he couldn't keep me the small child he held on his knee, or whose hair he ruffled, for ever. It wasn't that I loved him the less. I didn't. But I'd begun to learn about loving generally, and in loving – there *is* choice.

I was very quiet for the rest of the week. I was polite and smiled, but I stayed inside myself, even with the people and the party at the school, and I dreaded the Saturday picnic.

But Sandie kept bubbling over about it.

'Bev's coming, too!' she told me. 'And bringing Dieter! It should be a laugh, Juanita! Barry says we may have to take two cars!'

Mrs Walker rushed around all Friday, making savoury pies and salads and packing them into boxes, and on Saturday morning I lay in bed, feeling useless and alone and wishing I could develop some more 'English' tummy.

'Come on, J.!' Barry pushed his head round the door. 'You're not even dressed yet and Maggie's here!' He winked conspiratorially.

That made me smile and as soon as he'd closed the door behind him I slid out of bed.

I'd bought some English clothes, not many – jeans, tops, a pretty blouse – but I suddenly felt short, fat and ugly again. I didn't want to outshine Maggie. I never could. But I *did* want to be different.

'And you are,' I assured myself in the mirror as I smeared on a little lipstick. 'In Stratford, perhaps you can walk away and pick up a Japanese tourist, so you won't be in the way of the others! They are all couples. You are you, and alone, which is the difference.'

I stuck my tongue out at myself, fluffed my hair back behind my ears and thought about dashing into the garden to pick a rose so I could wear it between my teeth to show how different I was!

But when I eventually dragged myself downstairs, hearing all the giggles and laughter, Elvira bounded towards me and I bent down to scratch her between the ears.

'She's coming, too,' an unfamiliar voice said quietly. 'Though apparently she gets car-sick, and I've been told it's up to you and me to keep an eye on her. I'm Sam Watson — Beverley's brother.'

I straightened, wondering why Barry, or Sandie, or Maggie — or all three of them — had thought I'd be such a nuisance on the outing I'd have to have a stranger provided to keep me quiet.

Then I smiled.

The boy leaning against the hall wall was older than me, but it was perfectly obvious from the look on his face *he* wasn't too sure about today, either!

'Juanita Alvarez.' I held out my hand formally.

'And you don't really want to go on this picnic, do you?' Sam said with sudden understanding.

'Not a great deal.' Perhaps because I was feeling the way I *was* feeling, I wasn't shy with him, and even when I realised we were now holding hands instead of shaking them, I didn't pull away.

'Never mind!' His smile made me think of Barry. 'Stratford's okay. We can let the other happy couples smooch in corners. You and I can go for healthy walks!

'Say!' he squeezed my hand more tightly. 'Isn't it great Maggie and Barry are engaged? Have you seen the ring yet?'

I'd completely forgotten that today was the day Barry was giving Maggie the ring, and I left Sam where he was and rushed blindly into the kitchen.

Mr and Mrs Walker were standing with glasses in their hands. Barry had his arm round Maggie's shoulders. Dieter and Bev were sitting at the table whispering between themselves, and Sandie and Joe were giving each other a hug in a corner.

'All's well that ends well!' Mr Walker was saying proudly, then he suddenly noticed me and gestured for me to join them. 'Juanita, I'd like you to meet my future daughter-in-law! Barry and Maggie are getting married. Show her the ring, Maggie!'

Maggie glanced at me from under her eyelashes. I think she'd already guessed I might've had something to do with all this. But then she smiled and held out her left hand.

The eight small diamonds clustered round their central diamond glittered in the sunlight.

'Congratulations,' I murmured, holding her finger-tips gingerly and trying to sound surprised.

'Thank you.' She suddenly separated from Barry, put her arms round me and hugged me. 'Thank you a million times!' she murmured. 'Barry told me what you did. We went to the house first last night! There were flowers everywhere! And a teddy-bear with a big blue bow round its neck! *And* champagne! Juanita,' she pulled me away from the others who were all talking together excitedly, 'if there's ever anything *we* can do for you, please just let us know. Promise?'

I nodded shyly. Then Barry started hurrying us out towards the cars, and it was only when I found that I was driving with Sam Watson that the shivery, lonely feeling crept over me again.

Chapter 17

Sam's car was old, he'd borrowed it from a friend, but it had a back seat that folded down and although Elvira obviously didn't like travelling on anything except her own four paws and whimpered to begin with, when I opened my window she sat behind me with her nose resting on the glass and sniffed at the passing fresh air.

We went what Sam called 'the pretty way' – out past the airport, through Henley and Oxford and past Blenheim Palace, then on to Shipston-on-Stour, whose name made me giggle, and finally into Stratford, itself.

Sam and I didn't talk much, I think we were both shy of each other, but at a road junction just inside the town he suddenly said, 'The bridge we're going over is Clopton Bridge. The guy who had it built back in the fifteenth century became Lord Mayor of London.'

He waited to pull out into the main line of traffic, then half-turned and grinned. 'Just thought I'd throw you that free piece of info!'

'I'm very grateful,' I said seriously, but I was smiling as I scratched Elvira's chin. 'You know this town well?'

'Reasonably,' he shrugged, then swung carefully over into the car and coach park. 'I'm at Warwick University, which isn't very far away. But there's always a lot going on here, particularly in the spring and summer with the theatre. Also,' he parked the car, switched off the engine and stretched thankfully, 'I've got to admit I just like wandering around by the river, or going along the field path to Shottery and taking another look at Anne Hathaway's cottage! I keep telling myself it's the kind of place I'd like to live in, so I could paint a great picture or write a great novel or something. But I know I never will!'

'Why not?' I asked shyly, watching him as he got

out and went round the back to open the doors for Elvira.

'I'm not the type.' He opened my door for me, too, and Elvira jumped up on me with both front paws, tail wagging crazily. 'Anyway, I'm supposed to be reading Political Science, and how many political scientists have you ever heard of who ever did anything other than talk a great deal?'

I didn't even know what Political Science was and I was just about to ask when the others all came screeching over from Barry's car to join us.

'What'll we do first?' Sandie jumped up and down excitedly and Elvira woofed. 'I want to go shopping!'

'I want to show Dieter Shakespeare's tomb in the church and explain all the local history,' Bev butted in.

'I want to go and sit in the Great Garden at New Place,' Maggie sighed happily, hanging on to Barry as if she were afraid he might suddenly disappear. 'It's peaceful there, and if nobody minds I really couldn't stand a lot of foot-slogging sightseeing! But what about Juanita? It's her day, after all.'

'Juanita?' Barry tightened his arm round his new fiancée and smiled at me. 'How d'you feel?'

'I – I will be fine.' I bent down to hide the way I was blushing and scratched Elvira's ears. 'You all please do what you most wish.'

Something that felt like tears pricked viciously at the back of my eyes, and I tried to tell myself that, *of course*, I would enjoy myself. But right at that minute, deep down, I wanted to be at home either in the pale room at the Walkers' – or better still – in my own room in Spain.

'Juanita and I are going to wander with Elvira,' I

suddenly heard Sam say firmly. 'I know this place better than the rest of you, and I'm sure she doesn't want to get mowed down by a lot of Americans looking for the meaning of *Hamlet* and taking photographs!

'We'll see you up by the church in a couple of hours. Okay?' Then before I could say or do anything he'd fastened Elvira's lead on to her collar, taken me by the arm and begun to walk me up somewhere called Bridge Street.

'We'll take a look at the birthplace, because you'd better be able to say you've been,' he murmured, 'then we'll head back down towards the theatre and have a drink at the Dirty Duck.'

'Dirty Duck?' I had to almost run to keep up with him.

'Yes!' He threw back his head and laughed – a good, full-sounding laugh that made my own mouth twitch up at the corners in spite of itself. 'Once upon a time it was called the Black Swan. God knows when its name got changed!'

In fact the rest of the day had a magic about it that wasn't just to do with the warm sunshine and the way the trees, which seemed to be everywhere, rustled their secrets in the wind from the river.

Sam was an easy person to be with. He didn't talk all the time or insist on pushing pieces of historical information down my throat. But the silences were friendly, comfortable silences, and I caught myself wishing more than once I'd met him when I first started my holiday.

'Y'know,' he took my hand quite naturally as we finally strolled through the Theatre Gardens to look across the Avon towards Holy Trinity Church, 'you're nice, Juanita. Bev said you were shy but very quick on the uptake, and as smart-assed women always frighten me, I wasn't really looking forward to meeting you at all. But you're not that kind of "smart", are you?' He squeezed my fingers and a lovely little shiver quicksilvered through me.

'I don't think I'm smart in the slightest,' I said softly, watching Elvira circle a yapping white poodle suspiciously. 'And I am not a woman — yet. I am only learning to be one.'

It was the truth and I wasn't looking for reassurances or compliments, but what Sam did next surprised me.

He stopped, took hold of my other hand and pulled me straight so I had to look up at him.

'Maybe not quite,' he murmured. 'But you're getting there fast. And when you finally make it, I've got a strong suspicion you're going to leave a lot of broken hearts behind you!'

Then with the chestnuts and the tall cultivated grasses dipping and dancing their heads towards us, he bent and kissed me.

It was the first time I'd been kissed so properly on the lips, and for half a second I panicked, wondering what to do; wondering how to breathe without sniffing and how to keep my nose well away from bumping into his nose when we stopped.

Then his arms went round me, I found my hands sliding up to touch his face and neck, as if they had a mind of their own, and I closed my eyes, letting myself float along with all the different brilliant colours happening inside my brain.

Nothing else mattered except that moment — and Sam.

All the other sights and sounds and smells and dreams and discoveries of England were driven away.

We could've been anywhere, in any time, and when we finally separated from each other a little we just stood there, smiling with ourselves.

'Come on,' he whispered gently, putting his arm round my shoulders and hugging me to him. 'We'd better go and find the others and have that picnic Mrs Walker packed.'

Barry gave me a very old-fashioned look when we wandered up the Avenue towards the church with Elvira trotting along on her lead beside us, and I felt myself flush slightly. He and Sam stayed outside with the dog, and when Maggie and I walked down the nave towards the chancel and Shakespeare's tomb she suddenly reached over and gave my wrist a quick, reassuring squeeze.

'I'm glad,' she whispered simply. 'I know Barry's got a theory that summer's fine while it's here but that when autumn comes it changes everything. Don't let it change you or the way you're feeling now, even if you never see Sam again after today.

'Maybe he's just another part of your summer, like all the rest of us. But he's the part that'll be worth remembering.'

I nodded slowly, understanding what she was trying to say. Then we smiled at each other and went forward towards the brass rail that separated Shakespeare's plaque from the other parts of the church.

The rest of the day was fun, too.

We ate the picnic under the trees in the Theatre Gardens, then Barry and Sam decided to drive back home through the Vale of Evesham.

We had tea near somewhere called Perrots Brook in a very olde worlde tea-shop that sold what Sandie called 'proper' scones, with cream and home-made strawberry jam, and by the time we got to Oxford I was almost nodding off to sleep.

'Enjoy yourself?' Sam asked gently as we turned on to the motorway. 'I have.'

'Mmm. It's been wonderful.' I reached across and touched his arm lightly but shyly. 'And thank you for giving me all your time during it.'

'I was glad to. Really glad to.' He glanced at me and smiled quickly. 'And I mean that. Perhaps we can go somewhere else while you're here? I'd like to take you. We could explore Richmond Park or Kew Gardens.'

'I,' I turned, partly to check that Elvira was all right in the back and partly so he wouldn't be able to see my face, 'would like that, too. But it is not possible. I go home in three days. A friend,' I tried clumsily to explain, 'is being engaged. This is important for her, and Mama and Papa think I will want to be there.'

'Don't you?' The motorway traffic was light and Sam cruised along in the inside lane. The others had hooted and waved past us ages ago.

'Yes. No. I don't know.' I left Elvira to sleep and twisted back in my seat again. 'It will be good to be home. It will be good to be with old friends. But I think I may find Spain not the way I left it.'

'You mean *you're* not the same as you were?' He turned off the radio which had been humming softly since we'd got back into the car.

'Yes,' I nodded. 'I am changing — have changed.

Perhaps you always do when you leave your own country for a time? I am scared,' I hadn't really said this to myself yet, but suddenly the words fell out, 'that I will find nothing familiar in the people I used to know. That they will be the same and I will be very different.'

'Probably.' Sam picked up my hand, which was lying on the seat between us, and stroked the back of it thoughtfully. 'But that isn't a bad thing. And one day you'll be able to come back. Then,' he laughed, *we'll* probably all seem the same, as if you've caught us in a time-warp!'

'It has been wonderful,' I swallowed hard, 'to catch some of you at all! I'll never forget today, Sam.'

He suddenly signalled, pulled over into a layby behind an enormous parked lorry, and switched the engine off.

'I won't forget it, either,' he murmured, unfastening both our seatbelts. 'I won't say you're the most beautiful girl in the world. The chances are you're not.' His arm reached out and I felt his fingers trace patterns on my cheek. 'But there's something about you that's very special. Maybe I'd better,' his other hand touched my shoulder and he pulled me round gently to face him, 'start studying Spain's political science! Just in case you do come back, or I come looking for you.'

'Will you?' I whispered, moving closer to him.

'I don't know,' he said honestly. 'We're both young. Maybe we'll forget all about each other the day after you leave. But I doubt it somehow.

'I doubt it,' he tilted my chin up to his, 'very much. You're like the story of the ugly duckling and the swan. At the moment your duck's feathers are still dull and every which way, but very soon they won't be and you'll sail along regally, knowing who you are and what you're doing and where you're going.

'When that happens,' he added sadly, 'I'll just be a shape in your memory.'

Then our lips met again and I clung to him, feeling a crazy excited happiness shining through the car like a million rainbows.

Chapter 18

Sam wouldn't come in when we got back to the Walkers', and it was Barry who managed to bring the whole day naturally to a close by saying he was taking Maggie out for a private celebration dinner and whatever anybody else did was up to them.

Dieter had to catch the train back to his hostel, and Sandie and Joe so obviously wanted to be alone that I simply said how tired I was, excused myself and slipped upstairs.

I wanted to sit in the shadows and hug Sam's magic to me.

Mama might be convinced that English boys were more knowing than Spanish ones, and I remembered her words about a kiss being of no importance – or all importance.

Sam's kiss, Sam's gentleness, the simple fact that Sam was Sam, had become important. He'd never be just a shape in my memory. He was more like a statue standing beside huge gates that open on to a path along which I'd eventually walk or stumble or run.

I didn't know if it was possible to love somebody truly after just one day, but something in my head as well as my heart kept whispering, 'Yes!'

I wouldn't cry for him when I left. I wouldn't mope over him the way I'd seen Katerine and Dolores mope over their summer romances.

Perhaps I wouldn't even tell them about him, I decided. I'd just carry him around with me, and when I was on my own, or unhappy, or confused I'd remember the Stratford day and the way things were.

Although I hadn't really expected to, I went to sleep very quickly and woke up with a start when someone pulled back the curtains and sunshine flooded the room.

Barry was standing at the bottom of the bed with an idiotic grin on his face, jigging from foot to foot.

'Guess what?' he almost giggled, sitting down suddenly.

'What?' I rubbed my eyes and tried to focus. 'You look as if you've been handed a million dollars!'

'Almost! Almost!' He really did giggle that time and I wondered hazily if he'd been drinking so early in the morning. 'Remember we left before the post arrived yesterday morning?'

I hadn't even noticed, but I nodded, trying very hard to wake up properly.

'Well, when I got back late last night – everybody was in bed – *this* was lying on the dresser in the kitchen!' He pulled a crumpled envelope out of his jeans pocket and pushed it across to me. 'I've done it, Juanita! I've got it! I'm in!'

I didn't even have to read the letter – in fact it was

all in such formal, complicated, old-fashioned English that I couldn't properly understand it anyway – because I could tell from the insane smile on his face that the job with the BBC had been finalised, and I flung my arms round his neck, hugging him and laughing along with him.

'Well, well!' The door suddenly opened. 'This is a very touching scene, I must say!' Sandie stood there with her hands on her hips, frowning at us. 'I thought it was *Maggie* big brother had got engaged to!'

'It is, you idiot!' I almost choked, then pulled away from Barry and tried to be serious. 'Does she know yet? Have you told her?'

'Yup!' Barry leapt up and did a little war-dance. 'In fact, I rang her at half-past three this morning, after I'd opened it. Then I went round to see her so she could read it herself in case I was hallucinating!'

'Hallucinating *what*?' Sandie perched on the edge of the chair, looking puzzled.

'I've got a job!' Barry turned to her and gave her a huge kiss. 'I wrote off for it ages ago, then I went for the interview last week, and they've just confirmed they want me! Mum and Dad are probably going to go bananas because I'm flunking out of college, but it'll mean I'll have a salary and Maggie won't have to work after Simon's born and . . .'

'*Simon*!' I squawked, lying back on my pillows and feeling weak with laughter.

'Well, Simon if he's a boy,' Barry blushed, 'and Gemma if she's a girl.'

Mrs Walker must've heard all the noise and wondered what on earth was happening because seconds after Sandie and I had tried to smother Barry with pillows she poked her head into the room, trying to make up her mind whether to have her face laugh or frown.

Sandie threw herself at her mother, then we all started talking together and by the time poor Mrs Walker had more or less managed to find out what was going on, Barry had slipped away, giving me a quick wave and a wink as he closed the door quietly behind him.

'Well,' Sandie's Mum fiddled with things on the dressing-table, 'maybe he's right. But it does seem an awful waste.'

'No.' I swung myself out of bed, surprised at the confident tone of my voice. 'Nothing is ever wasted. For Barry, now, this is right. In time,' I pulled on my jeans and fastened them, 'he can go back to college if he needs or wants to. But with his job, he will be training and learning anyhow, and will not be full of guilts for his family. That is more important, don't you think?'

They both looked at me curiously and I wondered if I'd said too much. Then Mrs Walker came across and gave me a quick hug.

'Yes,' she murmured. 'That *is* more important. I wish, Juanita, that I knew my children as well as you seem to have got to know them in the very short time you've been here. We're all going to miss you when you leave. You've been exactly the breath of fresh air this family needed.'

Then she gave a happy gurgle of laughter and almost ran out of the room to tell her husband the news.

'Well,' Sandie watched me as I began to pack one or two things into my case, 'you've certainly made a hit around here, haven't you?'

I looked up at her quickly, wondering if she was going to be nasty again, but she had a broad grin on her face and her eyes were dancing just as much as Barry's feet had been earlier.

'Incidentally,' she said to me later when we were wandering across the common with Elvira, 'don't make any arrangements for Tuesday night, will you? We're having one or two people round. Just a sort of – well, goodbye party, if you like.'

'Oh no!' A cold shiver suddenly rocked my stomach. 'Not like the "hello" party? Not with Robin Derwent and all those other friends?'

'Of course not!' She linked her arm through mine and waved airily. 'Who's Robin Derwent, anyhow? This is just the family, and Joe, and Dieter and Bev – and Sam, of course.' She glanced at me mischievously through her eyelashes. 'We thought you'd like that. If the weather's decent there'll be a barbecue in the garden, so there isn't going to be a lot of fuss.'

I breathed a sigh of relief. The last thing I wanted was *any* kind of fuss. In a way, I simply wished I could disappear and leave everybody with their happy endings so I could start looking towards tomorrow and my own future.

Papa was going to be surprised when I told him I wanted to study languages and maybe even come back to England for the entire summer next year.

Mama would worry and wonder and ask endless questions about Barry, and if I mentioned Sam at all she would know immediately what had happened with him and worry even more.

Katerine would giggle, then tell me all about how wonderful it was to be engaged to Paco, and would probably bore me to death with stories of the kind of apartment they were saving to buy, and how she'd always known Paco was the only person in the world for her. Maybe he was, but only a lot of time would tell that.

I watched Elvira chasing round and round in circles with two other dogs and smiled to myself, trying to picture the common covered in fallen leaves or drifts of snow. Somehow I couldn't. In my mind it would always be a golden summer common where people played cricket, and couples lay in the grass, and dogs ran after bouncing rubber balls.

Chapter 19

On Monday, I said goodbye to Miss Ellen and the other students who'd been in my class but were staying on for a further two weeks.

'You did very well in your short time,' Miss Ellen said, handing me a certificate to prove I'd actually gone to the school and learned *something*! 'Keep it up when you get home, Juanita. You seem to have a natural ear. Try to find someone who'll carry on teaching you English as a foreign language. I hope you've been happy here?'

'Very.' I felt shy and clumsy. I'd bought her a special candle in the square shape of a country cottage, with windows and a door and even window-boxes, because it reminded me of the places we saw near Rye, but as I pushed it into her hands I had to swallow hard to stop silly tears spilling over. 'Perhaps, next year if Papa allows, I will come again.'

'Perhaps you will.' She patted my cheek gently, thanked me for her present, then, as if she knew how embarrassed I was feeling, said she had to go to a staff conference and hurried away.

I walked slowly out of the school and up Regent Street to Oxford Circus where I was meeting Sandie and Mrs Walker. Mrs Walker had promised to help me buy a cardigan for Papa and something special and pretty for Mama.

Everywhere was crowded. The shops seemed to be almost bursting at their seams with foreigners like me, and I found myself wondering what different memories all the other tourists would take home from England.

On Tuesday I did the rest of my packing and cleaned up my room as much as I could. Barry and Maggie were taking me to the airport in the morning, but the check-in time for the flight was early and I wanted to be ready well in advance.

I was sitting at the dressing-table wondering what to wear for my 'farewell' party — somehow nothing I had seemed suitable, all of it belonged to the old Juanita, not this new nervous one whose eyes had an unaccustomed sparkle at the thought of seeing Sam again — when the door opened and Sandie said, 'Shut your eyes and open your hands! It's surprise time!'

'What?' I half-turned on the stool, frowning. But Sandie waggled her finger at me crossly.

'Do what you're told. Shut your eyes and open your hands,' she repeated firmly. 'And no peeping! It's against the rules!'

I laughed, then closed my eyes, feeling an absolute

idiot, and finally felt someone put a large box across my arms.

'Okay. You can look now!'

Sandie, Bev, Mrs Walker and Maggie were all standing in the centre of the room smiling at me.

I stared at them. Then I stared down at the box. Then I just sat very still, blinking and not sure what to do next.

'Open it, twit!' Sandie yelled. 'It's for you!'

'From all of us,' Mrs Walker said softly.

'And we hope you like it,' Bev added, grinning.

Maggie didn't say a word. She simply came over, squatted down beside me and undid the first bit of the gift-wrapping.

'Now,' she murmured, 'you're on your own! And if I were you, I'd hurry up before the others lynch you!'

I slid my fingers underneath the sticky tape, peeled away the paper, lifted the lid from the cardboard box – and then gasped.

Lying folded on a bed of tissue paper was a white dress with a simple, heart-shaped neckline and a skirt trimmed in broderie-anglaise.

I shook it out, hardly able to believe it, then stood up, holding it against me, and spun round to look at my reflection in the mirror.

'It – it's beautiful!' I breathed.

'And it should be your size,' Mrs Walker said matter-of-factly. 'We "borrowed" one of your old ones and the shop assistant acted as our model! Try it on. Then when you're ready, come down to the garden. We'll all be waiting for you.'

I didn't know what to do. I was shaking. Part of me wanted to laugh and hug them all, and the other part wanted to burst into tears. I'd never had anything so lovely and so sophisticated in my life!

'Go on!' Maggie gave me a little push, then handed me another smaller box that she'd been hiding behind her back. 'And these should match as well. I just hope they fit!' Then she shooed everybody else out and left me hugging the dress and the other parcel.

Maggie's gift was a pair of silver, high-heeled, strappy sandals, and when I eventually went downstairs, I felt like Cinderella on her way to the ball.

I stood shyly in the kitchen doorway watching all the strangers who'd suddenly become friends talking and laughing as Mr Walker tried to get the barbecue to go, then I walked slowly forward, brushing my hair away from my face and knowing I would never, never forget this moment as long as I lived.

Barry wolf-whistled, then rushed to open a bottle of sparkling wine.

Dieter stood absolutely still, as if he'd suddenly taken root and was growing there.

Mrs Walker grabbed Elvira, who was trying to launch herself at me, by the collar and smiled.

Sandie, Joe and Bev all clapped, then Barry handed Sam a glass to give me and as our hands touched it was as if the rest of the world disappeared.

'You look – amazing,' Sam murmured while I sipped the fizzy wine. 'I was wrong about your duck's feathers. They've vanished already.'

'No.' I shook my head and smiled at him. 'Underneath, they are still there. This is a – what do you call it? – an optical illusion. This is not Juanita Alvarez. She has left for the day and allowed me to borrow her instead!'

'Pity.' The warmth in Sam's eyes was unmistakable. 'I quite liked her. But if you're her stand-in, I suppose I'll just have to put up with you for the party somehow! Now come on,' he took me by the elbow and led me forward, 'as the guest of honour you're to have Mr Walker's first overcooked sausage followed probably by his first undercooked hamburger!'

I laughed then and the stupid knot of tension I'd been feeling ran away into the shadows.

Sandie turned on the stereo and Dieter uprooted himself long enough to ask me to dance, but before I could even answer Barry had tapped him on the shoulder and with a mock scowl said, 'This one's mine!' Then he grabbed my hand, put his other arm round my waist and twirled me down the garden.

'Looking forward to being home?' he asked as I leaned, panting and laughing against one of the trees.

'I don't know.' I gulped and was suddenly serious. 'In many ways. But I will miss you all so much.

'Spain,' I shrugged, fumbling for words, 'is not like this. The people, my friends, are not like you. They are,' I tried to indicate what I meant by narrowing my hands together, 'smaller somehow, in their ideas. And there does not seem to be the freedom you all have here to go and change yourself into someone else if you feel like it.

'I expect,' I smiled up at him, 'I will become used to it again. But I'll never forget this summer.'

'No.' Barry's own face turned suddenly serious. 'I doubt if any of us will. But the good things,' he was fumbling in his back pocket and looking confused, 'will be worth remembering.

'This,' he pulled out a tattered brown paper bag and carefully took something from it, 'is from Maggie and me. I know, I know,' he held up his hand, 'she gave you the shoes, but they were from her, personally. This is from us both. Face forward!'

Puzzled, I did what I was told, then felt Barry's cool fingers gently fasten something round my neck.

'It isn't much,' he muttered as I fingered the chain, 'because you know better than anybody we can't afford much. But we wanted you to have it with love – and for luck. Also, my dear *fiancée*,' he said the word so proudly as Maggie came across, and then took her by the hand, 'said it would work well with the dress.'

I didn't know what to say. I kissed them both, then rushed through to the hall to look at myself.

The small crystal drop on the end of the gold chain sparkled and danced in the light from the table-lamp.

'It's a wish-stone,' I murmured aloud. 'Whenever things are going very wrong, whenever Papa and I are fighting, or I have forgotten to stone the olives for Mama and she is shouting at me, I shall put it on and wish – and everything will be all right again!'

Strange-feeling tears prickled at my nose and eyes. I didn't really want to cry, but the tears were good tears and one of them escaped and settled, as I watched myself, on the edge of my cheek, sparkling like the wish-stone.

'I'm looking for a lady,' a voice said softly, 'who does duck impressions. You don't happen to have seen her, do you?' Then two arms went round my waist and I leaned back against Sam, closing my eyes and trying to stop my heart skipping about with excitement and happiness.

He kissed my neck gently, then turned me to face him.

'You can't just run away, you know,' he

murmured. 'This party's in your honour. Mr Walker's almost set fire to the entire garden, the fizzy wine's getting warm, and poor Elvira has a very unhappy look about her. It could be,' he added thoughtfully, trying to keep his voice light, 'because she pinched a raw sausage. Or it could be,' he suddenly pulled me closer, 'because you're going away tomorrow. She'll miss you. We'll all,' he kissed me, 'miss you.'

'And I'll miss you.' I clung to him, biting my lip.

'I – I brought you something.' He handed me a small tissue-wrapped package. 'I saw it in a second-hand shop this morning. It made me think of you.'

I unwrapped the package carefully, realising my hands were shaking and knowing that if anyone else was nice to me I'd *really* break down and cry.

A small glass swan swam in the palm of my hand.

'Oh Sam!' I didn't know what to say. 'It's beautiful.'

'So is a certain duck I know, though where she's got to tonight I can't imagine!' He hugged me again and smiled. 'Now come on. No tears. No big emotional goodbyes. Meeting people and loving them isn't about that.'

'And autumn always comes,' I whispered, reaching up and putting my arms round his neck as if they belonged there.

'So does winter. So does spring. then it's back to summer again.' Our foreheads were touching. 'They're all different, but they're all as important as each other. It depends whom you meet during them.'

'Yes.' I touched the wish-stone, then buried my face in Sam's shoulder. 'And it's been a lovely summer!'

Going Back

The plane turned slowly and she looked down at the collection of dolls' houses and miniature duck ponds. The Thames seemed to snake gracefully through them all like a calm silver ribbon, as if it were tying them up and tucking them away to keep them safe.

Barry had said that she would probably fly over the house and the common, and she craned her neck, imagining that what could've been a large fluffy dog was Elvira chasing sticks and finding mysteries in the long grass.

She still wore the white dress. Somehow she wanted Papa to see a princess when she stepped off the plane.

The wish-stone glinted in the early afternoon light and she cradled the glass swan in her lap, staring down at it and seeing in its coloured eyes so many other sets of eyes.

Sandie – angry, frightened, crying, laughing.

Barry – tired, worried, happy, loving.

Dieter – very proper, very correct, very shy. How would he feel when his summer was over and he was back in Germany? Would he write to Bev? Would she write to him so they corrected the world between them?

And Sam! Tall, slightly odd-shaped Sam, who'd understood her loneliness – probably because he was lonely himself, she thought with a sudden flash of insight. Would she ever see Sam again, apart from in the glass swan? And somehow, whether she did or not didn't seem to really matter. In his own way, he'd always be there.

She hadn't told him she'd write. When they'd finally said goodbye after the party with its special cake that Sandie and Bev had made, she hadn't wanted to make that kind of promise. It had seemed too much of a commitment for either of them. Her swan's feathers were only temporary. In another few hours, in her own room with the sound of the sea outside, she'd automatically be turned back into an ugly duckling.

The *No Smoking* sign flashed off. People fumbled to undo their seatbelts, dragged out paperbacks and magazines, and above the steady hum of the engines conversation rippled and died.

She looked down through the cabin window again, trying to catch a last glimpse of the toy-town where she'd lived. Already it was something so far away it was hard to believe it had ever existed.

She closed her eyes and leaned back as the plane rose above the clouds and even the Thames disappeared.

She hadn't waved to Prince Charles. She hadn't even seen Prince Charles!

She'd only shopped in the King's Road once, and then she hadn't bought anything.

She'd slapped a boy's face in Covent Garden. She giggled suddenly, wondering what Dolores and Katerine would make of that. Most probably, they wouldn't believe her. Juanita Alvarez *never* went around slapping people's faces.

Juanita Alvarez was a little overweight, on the short side and had black hair that she kept cutting when her Papa wasn't looking. She was shy and insecure and just sixteen.

Nobody would ever believe that *that* Juanita

could've been sent red roses, even if she hadn't wanted them, or been likened to a beautiful regal swan by a boy who'd held her and kissed her as if she were the most important thing in his entire world.

She sighed, touching the wish-stone. Maggie had told her it would bring her back to them all one day and Sandie had said gloomily, as she'd waved goodbye at the gate, that nothing was going to be the same now Juanita was leaving.

That part, at least, was true. Nothing ever could be the same. Strangers had touched her life and pulled her in to share theirs with her.

She wondered how truly peculiar she was going to feel at home, and how out of place. But then she smiled mischievously sideways and winked at the sunlight. It seemed to wink back.

Whatever she was – whoever she was growing into – she'd just begun to realise that the person she turned into in the end would be a person she'd created for herself.

After autumn and winter, there'd always be spring, and another summer, full of their own surprises, grinning and waving wickedly from some other corner.

Ann de Gale
Island Encounter £1.25

Nic was a rebel. A rebel against her school-mates' endless hunt for boyfriends – and she tried to rebel when her charming but irresponsible father offered to take her camping in Corfu, on a holiday for single parents and their children. In spite of her reluctance, Nic went to Corfu, on a holiday for single parents and their children. In spite of her reluctance, Nic went to Corfu, and soon fell under the spell of the gnarled olive trees, the craggy rocks and the sea. She fell under the spell, too, of a solemn Scots boy she called Hamish . . .

Pam Lyons
Danny's Girl 85p

For sixteen-year-old Wendy, life was pretty straightforward. She enjoyed her tomboy existence with her parents and brother Mike on their farm in Norfolk. Then, late one sunny September afternoon, Danny wandered into her life and suddenly Wendy's happy and uncomplicated world is turned upside-down. Unsure of how she should behave or what is expected of her, she allows herself to be carried along in Danny's wake, and when he finds himself in trouble at his exclusive boarding school she is his only ally. Eventually, Wendy's fierce loyalty to the boy she loves leads them both deeper and deeper into trouble . . .

Mary Hooper
Follow that Dream £1.25

Her parents' dream of moving to Cornwall is a nightmare blow for Sally. How could she bear to leave London and be stuck away in the country . . . with no mates, no music, no decent clothes, no parties and no Ben, just when she was getting somewhere with him? But the long-awaited visit from her best friend, Joanne, brings some unexpected conflicts and Sally finds her determination to remain apart slowly undermined by the presence of a boy called Danny . . .

Fiction

☐	**The Chains of Fate**	Pamela Belle	£2.95p
☐	**Options**	Freda Bright	£1.50p
☐	**The Thirty-nine Steps**	John Buchan	£1.50p
☐	**Secret of Blackoaks**	Ashley Carter	£1.50p
☐	**Lovers and Gamblers**	Jackie Collins	£2.50p
☐	**My Cousin Rachel**	Daphne du Maurier	£2.50p
☐	**Flashman and the Redskins**	George Macdonald Fraser	£1.95p
☐	**The Moneychangers**	Arthur Hailey	£2.95p
☐	**Secrets**	Unity Hall	£2.50p
☐	**The Eagle Has Landed**	Jack Higgins	£1.95p
☐	**Sins of the Fathers**	Susan Howatch	£3.50p
☐	**Smiley's People**	John le Carré	£2.50p
☐	**To Kill a Mockingbird**	Harper Lee	£1.95p
☐	**Ghosts**	Ed McBain	£1.75p
☐	**The Silent People**	Walter Macken	£2.50p
☐	**Gone with the Wind**	Margaret Mitchell	£3.95p
☐	**Wilt**	Tom Sharpe	£1.95p
☐	**Rage of Angels**	Sidney Sheldon	£2.50p
☐	**The Unborn**	David Shobin	£1.50p
☐	**A Town Like Alice**	Nevile Shute	£2.50p
☐	**Gorky Park**	Martin Cruz Smith	£2.50p
☐	**A Falcon Flies**	Wilbur Smith	£2.50p
☐	**The Grapes of Wrath**	John Steinbeck	£2.50p
☐	**The Deep Well at Noon**	Jessica Stirling	£2.95p
☐	**The Ironmaster**	Jean Stubbs	£1.75p
☐	**The Music Makers**	E. V. Thompson	£2.50p

Non-fiction

☐	**The First Christian**	Karen Armstrong	£2.50p
☐	**Pregnancy**	Gordon Bourne	£3.95p
☐	**The Law is an Ass**	Gyles Brandreth	£1.75p
☐	**The 35mm Photographer's Handbook**	Julian Calder and John Garrett	£6.50p
☐	**London at its Best**	Hunter Davies	£2.90p
☐	**Back from the Brink**	Michael Edwardes	£2.95p

☐	**Travellers' Britain**	Arthur Eperon	£2.95p
☐	**Travellers' Italy**		£2.95p
☐	**The Complete Calorie Counter**	Eileen Fowler	90p
☐	**The Diary of Anne Frank**	Anne Frank	£1.75p
☐	**And the Walls Came Tumbling Down**	Jack Fishman	£1.95p
☐	**Linda Goodman's Sun Signs**	Linda Goodman	£2.95p
☐	**The Last Place on Earth**	Roland Huntford	£3.95p
☐	**Victoria RI**	Elizabeth Longford	£4.95p
☐	**Book of Worries**	Robert Morley	£1.50p
☐	**Airport International**	Brian Moynahan	£1.95p
☐	**Pan Book of Card Games**	Hubert Phillips	£1.95p
☐	**Keep Taking the Tabloids**	Fritz Spiegl	£1.75p
☐	**An Unfinished History of the World**	Hugh Thomas	£3.95p
☐	**The Baby and Child Book**	Penny and Andrew Stanway	£4.95p
☐	**The Third Wave**	Alvin Toffler	£2.95p
☐	**Pauper's Paris**	Miles Turner	£2.50p
☐	**The Psychic Detectives**	Colin Wilson	£2.50p

All these books are available at your local bookshop or newsagent, or can be ordered direct from the publisher. Indicate the number of copies required and fill in the form below   12

....

Name_____
(Block letters please)

Address_____

_____

Send to CS Department, Pan Books Ltd, PO Box 40, Basingstoke, Hants
Please enclose remittance to the value of the cover price plus:
35p for the first book plus 15p per copy for each additional book ordered
to a maximum charge of £1.25 to cover postage and packing
Applicable only in the UK

While every effort is made to keep prices low, it is sometimes
necessary to increase prices at short notice. Pan Books reserve
the right to show on covers and charge new retail prices which
may differ from those advertised in the text or elsewhere